P9-BBT-631

CHASING HELICITY

INTO the WIND

Also by Ginger Zee

Chasing Helicity

CHASING HELICITY

INTO the WiND

GINGER Zee

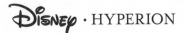

DISNEP · HYPERION

Los Angeles   New York

Copyright © 2019 by Ginger Zee

All rights reserved. Published by Disney • Hyperion, an imprint of Disney Book Group. No part of this book may be reproduced or transmitted in any form or by any means, electronic or mechanical, including photocopying, recording, or by any information storage and retrieval system, without written permission from the publisher. For information address Disney • Hyperion, 125 West End Avenue, New York, New York 10023.

Printed in the United States of America

First Hardcover Edition, April 2019
10 9 8 7 6 5 4 3 2 1
FAC-020093-19067

Names: Zee, Ginger, author.
Title: Into the wind : chasing Helicity / Ginger Zee.
Description: First hardcover edition. • Los Angeles ; New York : Disney-Hyperion, an imprint of Disney Book Group, 2019. • Summary: While visiting her friend Mia in Texas and helping at Aunt Suze's bed and breakfast, Helicity Dunlap gets caught in a derecho and loses track of her older brother, Andy.
Identifiers: LCCN 2018022386 (print) • LCCN 2018028104 (ebook) • ISBN 9781368045872 • ISBN 9781368002172
Subjects: • CYAC: Bed and breakfast accommodations—Fiction. • Windstorms—Fiction. • Meteorology—Fiction. • Weather—Fiction. • Storm Chasers—Fiction. • Family life—Texas—Fiction. • Texas—Fiction.
Classification: LCC PZ7.1.Z42 (ebook) • LCC PZ7.1.Z42 Tro 2019 (print) • DDC
  [Fic]—dc23

Visit www.DisneyBooks.com

SUSTAINABLE FORESTRY INITIATIVE
Certified Sourcing
www.sfiprogram.org
SFI-00993

THIS LABEL APPLIES TO TEXT STOCK

For my twister number two, Miles

CHAPTER ONE

"So, Felicity, are you ready for your first flight?"

Helicity Dunlap suppressed a sigh and turned to the woman in the severely starched airline uniform sitting beside her. JULIE, her name tag said. An airline chaperone, she was in charge of Helicity for the duration of the flight from Grand Rapids to Houston. There, she would hand her off to Helicity's best friend, Mia, and Mia's aunt. Julie seemed nice enough, even if she hadn't gotten her name right.

"It's *Hel*icity," she said patiently. "With an *H*."

Julie peeked at Helicity's paperwork. "Huh. I

assumed that was a typo, just another airline mistake. You know, like the food." She changed her voice to sound like a cheesy stand-up comedian. "Airline food—what's up with that?"

Helicity cringed inwardly at her chaperone's attempted humor. Outwardly, she offered Julie a polite smile.

Julie resumed her normal voice. "*Helicity*. I've never heard that before. Is it a family name?"

Helicity was as used to this question as she was to people getting her name wrong, so she had a ready answer. "My grandmother was a physicist. She studied helicity. I got the name because my mom liked the sound of the word, which means to spin, basically." The real definition of *helicity* was much more complex, but she'd learned long ago not to elaborate. Most people tended to glaze over when she did.

Further discussion was cut short by the announcement that the plane was ready for takeoff.

Julie grinned. "Here we go!"

The engines powered up with a high-pitched whine. A second later, the plane shot forward down the runway. As the G-force from the rapid acceleration pushed her back into her seat, Helicity instinctively reached for the necklace she always wore—a lightning bolt on a long chain. It wasn't hers; it belonged to her mentor, Lana McElvoy. Lana, who was still in a coma in a hospital. Because of her. Because of Helicity.

Her hand tightened around the charm's jagged edges as the wheels bumped on the tarmac. Then the wheels left the earth behind, and the plane soared on a sharp incline into the sky.

Helicity pushed aside her bangs and curled up closer to the small oval window. She had recently given herself a super-short, shoulder-length bob haircut that swept across her forehead. She'd done a decent job, but the new style made her look much older, and her mother had been startled when she saw it. Helicity had needed to make the change, just as she'd needed to take her horse, Raven, for long solo rides in the countryside surrounding her hometown and to travel hundreds of miles to Texas. Anything and everything to avoid running into her past.

Outside the window, the ground below vanished in a shroud of pale gray mist.

I'm inside a cloud, Helicity realized.

Seconds later, the plane burst through the foggy layer and into the brilliant blue sky above. She blinked at the sudden brightness. Then her eyes adjusted, and her breath caught in her throat.

A carpet of puffy stratocumulus clouds stretched in endless waves toward the horizon. The late afternoon sunshine painted the expanse with warm golden tones. The only thing missing from the fairy-tale landscape was a palace gleaming in the distance.

Helicity was enthralled. She loved anything to do with clouds. Anything to do with the weather in general, in fact, which was why she dreamed of becoming a meteorologist and storm chaser one day. While many kids her age spent their free time staring at screens, Helicity scanned the world around her for evidence of atmospheric and environmental change. Things like trees bending in the wind and grassy fields parched to brown from lack of rain. Shimmering heat creating that beautiful mirage, radiating up from the pavement, and sunlight softened by low-hanging haze. Slick patches of black ice lying in wait for unwary travelers and powdery snow skimming across frozen expanses. Each day, the ever-changing conditions delivered something new and amazing, and Helicity didn't want to miss a single moment.

Or at least, that's how she felt until two terrifying storms—first a tornado, then a flash flood—caught her and those she loved in their powerful clutches. Her parents had lost everything in the tornado. Her brother, Andy, had risked his life to search for her during that same terrible storm. And Lana—

"It's beautiful, isn't it?"

Julie broke into Helicity's thoughts. Helicity blinked, then lifted a shoulder and let it drop. "Oh, yeah . . . it's nice."

"I've seen views like that hundreds of times," Julie continued. "One of the perks of working for the airline, you know?"

Helicity knew Julie was trying to engage her in conversation. But since the flood, she hadn't been sleeping well, and she just didn't have the energy to feign interest in small talk. So, after offering the chaperone a smile and a nod, she closed her eyes, intending to pretend she'd dozed off.

Soon, though, the plane's gentle rocking motion

and the steady drone of the engines lulled her into her first real sleep in weeks.

It didn't last long. The nightmares intruded, a familiar montage of disturbing images, some real, some fabricated by her overactive mind. Her mother cowering in the basement as the tornado ripped their home apart. Her father staring in anguish at his son's battered body. Lana mouthing something Helicity couldn't hear over the roar of the floodwaters. Andy wide-eyed with terror as his car flipped, rolled, bounced—

She woke with a gasp. The bouncing was no dream.

Turbulence. The word flashed through her mind as the plane gave another shudder.

Turbulence, she knew, was caused by sudden changes in the airflow around the plane, like a jetty in the ocean that disrupts the flow of ocean waters. Turbulence could be caused by so many different factors: nearby storms, proximity to mountain ranges, and alterations in the jet stream. There weren't any mountains nearby, and she didn't see any thunderstorms, so it had to be clear-air turbulence.

Knowing what caused the plane to shake was one

thing. Experiencing that shaking was something very different.

The shuddering stopped, then began again, more intensely this time. A tone sounded, and the FASTEN SEAT BELT sign flashed on. A finger of unease crawled up Helicity's spine. "Is this normal?" she asked Julie.

A lurch sent the chaperone's drink splashing into her lap. "Oh, sh—sugar," she amended in mid-expletive. She mopped at the mess with her tiny airline napkin, then shoved the sodden wad into her plastic cup. "I'll be right back."

Ignoring the seat belt sign, she unbuckled and headed to the galley. Suddenly, the plane gave a violent jerk. Julie stumbled. Helicity was thrown sideways in her seat. Her head hit the window, and she saw stars. When her vision cleared, she saw Julie had strapped herself into the plane's jump seat.

The loudspeaker crackled. "Ladies and gentlemen," the pilot calmly intoned, "as you have no doubt noticed, we are experiencing a bit of turbulence. At this time, we ask—"

His request was cut short when the plane suddenly plummeted like an elevator in free fall. Cries of alarm filled the cabin as Helicity and the other passengers went weightless for a split second. Then, like a yo-yo reaching the end of its string, the descent halted abruptly. Helicity nearly bit her tongue when she thudded back down into her seat.

Without warning, an overhead compartment popped open. A child's pink backpack tumbled out and hit the man sitting below. Cursing, he kicked it under the seat in front of him, then half-stood, twisting awkwardly to re-secure the latch.

"Sir! Sit down!" the attendant commanded.

Too late! The plane lurched again. The man flew backward into the aisle. A second jolt sent him sprawling forward. His nose cracked against the metal armrest. He howled and clapped a hand over his face. Blood gushed between his fingers and down his chin as he dragged himself back into his seat.

Helicity's fear spiked. She gripped the lightning bolt with both hands. Her palms were slick with sweat, but her mouth was bone-dry, her breath coming in ragged gasps.

I'm a survivor, not a victim. I'm a survivor, not a victim.

Out of nowhere, her mind conjured up the mantra that had pulled her back from the brink in the past. Some people might use the words *survivor* and *victim* interchangeably, but to her, their meanings were very different. Survivors pushed their way through adversity; victims were defined by it. Given a choice, she'd choose to be a survivor every time.

She latched on to the words, willing them to force out the adrenaline-fueled panic pulsing through her system. She breathed as Lana had once taught her, slow and deep, in through her nose and out through her mouth. She focused on the necklace digging into her palm—a sensation she could control and that could ground her.

I'm a survivor, not a victim.

The whine of the engines sliced into her thoughts. The plane nosed higher into the sky, aiming to rise above the turbulence. She sensed the passengers around her holding their breath. The craft jostled a few more times. Then, finally, the ride smoothed out.

A murmur of relief washed through the cabin.

"Who says Disney has the best rides?" the pilot

joked over the loudspeaker. His comment elicited a smattering of shaky, forced laughter.

Helicity slowly released her death grip on the necklace.

Julie hurried down the aisle. "You all right, Fel— *Hel*icity? I hope you weren't scared."

A sunbeam struck the lightning bolt, making it wink and flash.

"No, I wasn't scared," she murmured. *I was terrified.*

CHAPTER TWO

T he plane taxied to a stop at the Houston terminal two hours later. Helicity was the first one out of her seat. Julie trotted to keep pace with her on the walk to the baggage carousel. "Wow, you must really be looking forward to seeing your friend!"

"Yeah, I—"

"Helicity!" A petite girl with short coal-black hair, a heart-shaped face, and a slightly upturned, sunburned nose pushed through a knot of people.

"Mia!" Helicity grabbed her friend in a bear hug. Mia squeezed her back with just as much ferocity.

A woman wearing loose-fitting linen shorts and an unbuttoned pink blouse over a white tank top joined them. She looked so much like Mia that Helicity knew she had to be her aunt, Suzette.

"I've got her from here," Suzette said to Julie. Julie checked her ID, then told Helicity good-bye and disappeared into the airport crowd.

"Well, Helicity." Mia's aunt cocked her head sideways, smiling. "If you don't mind my saying so, you look like you've been through the wringer."

Helicity almost told them about the turbulence and her panic attack. But she held her tongue. It wasn't something she wanted to think or talk about right then.

"The flight was a little bumpy, Suzette," she replied instead.

"Bummer. And call me Suze. Everyone does. And speaking of calling," she added, "phone your folks so they know you're safe and sound."

The carousel began spitting out luggage just as Helicity finished talking to her mother. She retrieved her single duffel with a tingle of pride when Suze nodded approvingly at how lightly she'd packed. She followed Mia and Suze to the parking garage, grateful to be leaving the airport behind and determined not to think about the return flight she would eventually have to take.

"Wait until you see our wheels," Mia murmured with a hint of laughter.

"Hey, now," Suze chided. "Don't go mocking the mighty beach-mobile." She waved her hand at a row of vehicles.

"The beach-mo— Oh." Helicity picked out their car right away. It was a massive four-seat ragtop convertible from the 1960s, as wide as a bus and so long its backside stuck partway into a second parking space. The body was a brilliant turquoise with chrome trim. The interior and ragtop were creamy white. "That is really . . . something."

"Most recognized car on all of Bolivar Peninsula," Suze said, patting the hood affectionately. "I've got another car back home, but I figured we'd pick you up in style."

They drove with the top down and their hair blowing in the wind. For a moment, Helicity felt as carefree as her hair and forgot about her troubles. About an hour in, they pulled over to grab ice cream and put the top of the beach-mobile up to enjoy a calmer end to the ride.

Darkness had fallen by the time they reached Port Bolivar, a small community on the southwest tip of Bolivar Peninsula. They pulled off the main highway onto a side street, then into a dirt parking area near Suze's bed-and-breakfast. Warm, humid air enveloped Helicity when she opened the car door. A light breeze carried the familiar scent of newly mown grass, sun-kissed dust, and car exhaust, plus something she'd never smelled before. She inhaled deeply, trying to identify it.

"That's the sea you're smelling," Mia told her. "Kind of different from the freshwater we're used to from Lake Michigan, huh?"

Helicity inhaled again and detected the salty tang. A hint of fish, too. Not bad fish like when her mom made homemade fish sticks, but good, fresh fish. The onshore breeze brought the sound of lapping waves. "How close are we to the beach?"

"You'll see," Mia said mysteriously. "But first . . ." She waved her arms. Warm yellow motion detector lights flicked on, illuminating the bed-and-breakfast's exterior. "Welcome to the Beachside!"

Helicity blinked in surprise. "It's on stilts!"

The beach house was unlike anything she'd ever seen in Michigan. Painted the same turquoise as the beach-mobile with white trim around the doors and windows, it stood on posts that raised it several feet above the ground. There were two sets of stairs, one from the parking area to the front of the house, the other to a large back deck. Beneath the house and deck was an open storage space with beach umbrellas, chairs, Boogie Boards, and a trio of bicycles with wicker baskets on the handlebars. In the far corner was an enclosed outdoor shower. A short distance away from the house was a stone fire pit surrounded by colorful Adirondack chairs.

Helicity took it all in as she followed Mia and Suze up the weathered back stairs to the deck. She assumed they were going inside, but Mia led her to the railing.

"Check it out," she said.

"Oh . . . wow," Helicity breathed.

The deck looked over the grassy expanse and the fire pit. The grass gave way to a small dune. A footpath cut through the dune to a sandy beach. And beyond that was the Gulf of Mexico. The full moon bathed the gently rippling waves with its silver-white glow.

"It's so beautiful," Helicity whispered.

"Yeah." Mia leaned her elbows on the railing and stared out at the view. "There's something special about this place, Hel. I feel so calm here. At peace, if that doesn't sound too hokey. Suze says it's because I'm away from the daily stress of my home life." She shrugged.

Helicity shot her a quick look. Mia's parents had gone through a nasty divorce the year before. Mia had been caught in the middle of it but had seemed to come out okay. Now Helicity wondered if she'd been hiding deeper feelings—feelings she wasn't ready to share, not even with her best friend.

I get that, she thought, thinking of her own reluctance to reveal her panic attack.

"Anyway, that's the main reason I invited you here," Mia continued. "I thought being someplace different, away from the constant reminders of—of everything you've been through, might help you, you know, heal a little bit."

Helicity slipped her arm around Mia's shoulders and gave her a quick hug. "Just being with you, seeing this"—she nodded at the moonlit seascape—"I already feel better."

CHAPTER THREE

A beam of sunshine woke Helicity the next morning. She blinked, momentarily confused by her unfamiliar surroundings. Then she saw Mia's empty bed and remembered.

Texas. I'm in Texas. Well, at least for now. Nothing was permanent. The tornado that had destroyed her hometown, the flash flood that had ripped Lana from her grasp, had taught her that.

She and Mia had talked late into the night. Or rather, Helicity had talked. Mia had listened, only interjecting exclamations of horror, requests for clarification, and bursts of indignation now and then.

"You must have been *terrified* when you heard those floodwaters coming!"

"Andy or your folks will keep you posted on how Lana's doing, then?"

"And Sam—he just *disappeared*?"

Mia's outrage had been fierce when Helicity mentioned Sam Levesque, a lean seventeen-year-old with spiky black hair and ice-blue eyes who shared Helicity's fascination with the weather. Lana had introduced them after the tornado. Helicity had felt an electric jolt zing through her the first time he smiled at her. Felt it every time after, too. She fought her insane attraction, though. Told herself that Sam was too old for her. Too reckless. A typical bad boy, complete with snarky, attitude-laden demeanor.

But, oh. Those brilliant blue eyes and that killer smile. Who was she kidding? He was so bad he was good. Not just good. He was irresistible. To her, anyway.

She'd been over the moon when Lana invited them both to join her and a fellow meteorologist named Ray on a summer-long storm-chasing expedition. The flash flood had ended that expedition. It might have ended Sam's life, too, if not for Helicity.

And mine, if Lana hadn't plunged into the waves to save me . . . Helicity pushed the memories from her mind and went to find Mia and Suze.

Helicity and Mia's bedroom was an enclosed second-story loft at the back of the house. It had its own tiny bathroom with a shower. Outside their door was a small landing with a half wall that overlooked a common room below. Like their loft, that wide-open space had a beachy theme—driftwood-gray-tiled floors, furniture in shades of white, blue, green, and tan, and decor that featured shells and sea glass. There were no guests at the bed-and-breakfast that day, so the common room was unoccupied, but she heard voices coming from the kitchen. She headed down the stairs, taking in the view of the Gulf through a large bank of picture windows.

She found Mia and Suze sitting at the kitchen island.

"'Morning, sleepyhead." Suze pushed a blueberry muffin across the granite slab. "Eat up, and then Mia and I will give you the lowdown on what happens around here. Sound good?"

Mouth full of muffin, Helicity nodded. Her parents had worked out an arrangement with Suze. In exchange for room and board, Helicity would do chores at the bed-and-breakfast. She was more than willing to work—anything to keep her mind from flashing back into memories. Or rather, those nightmares.

After breakfast, she got the Beachside tour. Besides the kitchen, common room, and Suze's master suite, there were three guest rooms on the first floor, each with two queen-size beds. One had a private bathroom; the other two shared a bath. Checkout time was no later than eleven in the morning and check-in was anytime after three.

"In between those hours," Mia said, "we clean the rooms top to bottom. Luckily, most people don't leave huge messes behind." She waggled her eyebrows. "What they do leave are nice tips." She gestured to a glass jar near the sink. "We can keep the money in there, then divvy it up before we go home, okay? Oh, and Tuesdays we have the day off because Suze doesn't book guests on Mondays."

"Otherwise," Suze added, "when you're done with

your housekeeping duties, your time is your own."

"I go treasure hunting on Crystal Beach most afternoons," Mia said, referring to the twenty-seven miles of shoreline that stretched along Bolivar Peninsula's south coast. "I want to find a shark tooth, but so far, all I've found is sea glass, shells, and a few crusty sea beans."

"Sea beans?" Helicity queried.

"Seeds and pods that travel the ocean currents and wash onto our shore," Suze explained. She pulled a map from a drawer and unfolded it on the kitchen island. It showed the Gulf of Mexico, a vast, misshapen oval of water almost entirely encircled with land. Texas, Louisiana, Mississippi, Alabama, and Florida curved around the top of the oval, with Mexico to the west and south, and the island nation of Cuba poking into the opening between Mexico's Yucatán Peninsula and the tip of Florida.

"A current of warm water flows up from South America, past Central America, through the Yucatán Channel, and into the Gulf." Suze traced her finger along the current's northward path. "Along the way, it picks up all kinds of stuff—trash, fishing nets, buoys, boat parts." She gave a wry smile. "You would not believe what washes ashore here after a big storm."

"But it also brings the sea beans," Mia put in.

Suze nodded. "Sometimes they're in the water so long, they get encrusted with barnacles or covered over with seaweed before the Bolivar Peninsula." She tapped the map on the tiny slice of land she called home.

Helicity was intrigued by the sea bean story. But she knew the current did a lot more than convey interesting seeds from faraway places.

She'd learned about the Gulf of Mexico and its currents from Lana during the storm-chasing expedition. They had stopped to refuel Lana's SUV and Ray's tricked-out vehicle, Mo West—short for Mobile Weather Station. While Lana and Ray were pumping gas, Sam ran into the station's convenience store. He emerged with snacks as well as a tiny bottle of something called N-R-Geee!

Lana made a face when she saw the bottle. "Do you know what's in that stuff? Besides chemicals, I mean?"

"A boost of energy," Sam said with a grin. "Or *liquid giddy-yap*, according to the commercials."

"Yeah, like you need more giddy-yap," Ray muttered, rolling his eyes.

"The contents of that little bottle will do to you," Lana warned, "what a current eddy does to a hurricane in the Gulf of Mexico."

"What's a current eddy?" Helicity asked.

Lana racked the gas nozzle and collected her receipt. "Hop in. I'll explain on the way to the hotel."

Sam punched Ray in the arm. "Guess that means I'm riding shotgun in Mo West!"

Ray swiped the N-R-Geee! out of Sam's hand. "Not with this, you're not."

Sam pulled a second bottle from his pocket and dangled it just out of Ray's reach. "Good thing I bought two."

Lana jerked her head in their direction. "Let's go before this gets ugly," she said to Helicity.

"Too late," Helicity responded.

In the SUV, Lana gave her a brief overview of the Gulf of Mexico's currents, and then moved on to the eddies.

"Every six months or so," she said, glancing over her shoulder before changing lanes, "a ring of warm, circulating water breaks away from the current, form-ing an eddy. The eddy meanders around the Gulf, happily spinning as it goes. Usually, it's not a big prob-lem. But if an eddy occurs during the Gulf's hurricane season, it can spell trouble. Do you know why?"

Helicity remembered how Lana had compared Sam's drink to the eddy. "That warm spinning water is a pocket of energy that could feed the storm," she guessed, "making the hurricane way more powerful than it originally was."

"Exactly," Lana said with an approving nod. "The Gulf isn't the only place current eddies occur. But with such a huge population so near its shorelines, eddies that form there can be real troublemakers if a hurricane hits."

Helicity looked back at Mo West trailing behind them. "Poor Ray. He's trapped with Hurricane Sam and his bottle of eddy."

To herself, she added that she would love to be trapped in a car with Sam.

She never suspected that days later, she would be. Trapped in the SUV. The floodwater rushing in. Sam's head bleeding. The life vests. The ropes. And the ambulance.

Then . . . silence. Sam had disappeared after the accident. Never checked on Lana, never cared to check on Helicity. The boy she had fallen in love with had vanished.

"Helicity? Hello? You still with us?"

Mia's voice prodded Helicity from her memory. "Sorry," she said. "Just thinking about sea beans."

 "**C**leaning rooms is way more fun with you here."

Mia handed Helicity a stack of clean towels from the linen supply, grabbed a pile of fresh sheets, and led the way back to a guest room.

A week had passed since Helicity arrived at the Beachside. She'd fallen easily into the daily routine—and just as easily into bed each night. "That's thanks to the combination of hard work and fresh sea air," Suze told her when she marveled about how soundly she'd been sleeping.

Helicity nodded, though she thought the truth lay elsewhere.

Mia had been right: she felt better being away from the stress back home. Her guilt over the danger Andy and Lana had put themselves in for her sake was still there, but it didn't weigh on her quite so oppressively. As for another panic attack, so far, nothing she'd encountered had triggered one.

Her new journal was helping her sort through her feelings, too. She hadn't planned to keep one. But her first afternoon in Texas, she, Mia, and Suze had taken the ferry from Bolivar Peninsula to Galveston Island. As the boat motored across the small channel that connected the Gulf of Mexico to Galveston Bay, a trio of bottlenose dolphins appeared. Their grace and agility, carefree abandon, and natural smiles sent a happy warmth through Helicity's veins. She wanted to hold on to that glow. So, when she spotted a journal with a dolphin on the cover, she bought it. She'd written in it nearly every night since.

She'd been less consistent communicating with her family. Not because she didn't miss them, but because the tension back home traveled right through the phone. Her town had been reduced to rubble by the tornado, her family home torn apart. Those losses were devastating, but it was Andy's uncertain future that had them on edge. The injuries he'd sustained while searching for her during the tornado had put a lucrative football scholarship in jeopardy. Without those funds, their parents couldn't afford to send him to college. Without college, his dream of playing professional football one day would die.

Their chores done, Helicity and Mia set off for the beach. Beneath the deck, Mia paused uncertainly next to the Boogie Boards. "You want to try these today?"

Back in Michigan, they had always been the first ones to jump in the pool or charge into the lake, even when the lake water felt as frigid as newly melted snow. But Helicity's first night there, Mia made a confession.

"I'm afraid to swim in the Gulf because I saw a dead shark on the beach. It freaked me out. I mean, Lake Michigan might be cold, but it doesn't have killer fish."

Helicity had been secretly relieved. She hadn't gone swimming since the flash flood. Whenever she got knee-deep in the waves, memories of other, more powerful ones sent her backpedaling to the safety of the sand. She didn't even like taking baths anymore. They weren't relaxing. Just the opposite, in fact: the water surrounding her was terrifying. She wanted to get past the phobia. But she wasn't ready to face that beast. Not yet.

"Beachcombing is fine with me," she said.

Beach buckets in hand, the girls headed down the dune path. The midafternoon sun beat down on them with the intensity of an open furnace as they searched for treasures along the shoreline. Suddenly, a commotion farther down the beach caught Helicity's attention. "What's going on?"

"One way to find out!"

Pails in hand, they hurried toward the tight group of people.

"We need to get help down here right away," a man yelled, "or she's going to die!"

Helicity's step faltered. Was there a *body* on the beach? Even through all of the recent tragedies, she still hadn't seen a dead body. She had seen Lana looking lifeless in the hospital bed, a tube down her throat breathing for her, and that was an image that would never leave her mind. Then the crowd parted, and she saw that "she" wasn't a person, but a stranded dolphin.

"Oh, no!" she cried.

Patches of sand encrusted the dolphin's smooth gray skin. The dorsal fin bore a distinctive mark—a white slash of a scar. It gave a weak beat of its tail flukes and puffed a gasp of breath from its blowhole. Helicity's heart broke to see the beautiful animal in such distress.

Someone produced a phone and called for help. "Marine mammal rescue says to keep her skin wet and covered," he instructed.

Helicity immediately emptied her bucket and charged into the surf. She ran back out with a pailful of seawater. When she neared the dolphin, she slowed and started murmuring in low, soothing tones. "You'll be okay. It's going to be okay. You're a survivor."

Please be a survivor, she added silently.

"Not so close!" a middle-aged woman fretted. "It might bite you!"

Mia stepped in front of her. "Dolphins don't bite. At least . . . I don't think they do." She looked over her shoulder at Helicity. "Go on. You got this."

Helicity eased closer to the dolphin. She tipped the bucket and trickled the water over its torso, taking care to avoid the blowhole.

The dolphin's black eye rolled to look up at her. She stared into its liquid depths, her breath catching as she recognized the intelligence there.

"Hey. Here's more."

A teenage boy with deeply tanned skin, blond curls, and a slight southern lilt sidled up behind her with another pail of water. She started to move out of his way, but he stopped her. "Nuh-uh." He handed her the bucket. "Like your friend said—you got this."

Helicity glanced back. Mia and the others had formed a bucket brigade, passing empty containers to the water and sending them back full. Wet beach towels, too, which the boy helped her drape over the dolphin's body.

Finally, the rescue unit arrived. She and the boy backed away to let the trained volunteers do their job.

"That was intense." The boy smiled broadly. His brown-black eyes were almost as dark as the dolphin's and even more intelligent. "I'm Trey, by the way."

"Helicity." She waited for the inevitable look of confusion, but Trey just nodded.

"Nice to meet you, Helicity."

He was strikingly handsome, she noted with an unexpected quickening of her pulse. It wasn't the zing she felt with Sam. This was different. This felt like she had known him for years. His easygoing demeanor, deep dimples, and slightly crooked, bright white smile created an aura of . . . joy. And she didn't even know him.

He was about to say something else when Mia came up behind them, tossing their beach buckets in the sand. The three talked in low tones while the rescue crew carefully loaded the dolphin onto a special stretcher, then floated the stretcher out to their waiting boat. One volunteer broke away to thank them for their help.

"What will happen to her?" Helicity asked.

"He, actually," the volunteer said. "We're bringing him to our rehabilitation center in Galveston. Hopefully, we'll figure out what's wrong with him, then get him strong enough to go back in the wild. You can watch his progress on our Facebook page, if you want." She excused herself to rejoin her crew.

"Facebook?" Mia chuckled. "Do people our age even use Facebook?"

Helicity shrugged. "I might sign up just to see the dolphin."

"I will if you will," Trey said, "and if we can be friends on it."

The hopefulness in his tone caught Helicity off guard. Suddenly flustered, she murmured, "Oh, um. Sure. What about you, Mia?"

Mia snorted. "Forget it. I'll just troll Suze's account instead. Speaking of Suze . . ." She stood. "It's almost time to start dinner."

"Oh." Trey sounded disappointed. "Well, see you."

"Yeah. See you." Mia waited a beat as if expecting Trey to do or say something more. When he didn't, she grabbed Helicity's hand and pulled her back toward home.

They'd just reached the dune path when Trey ran up behind them. He was taller than Helicity had realized. Broad-shouldered, too, with a sheen of sweat that made his skin gleam like polished bronze. Heat rose to her cheeks when she realized she was staring, and she quickly looked away.

"You forgot these." He held out the buckets.

Helicity was embarrassed. Buckets. They seemed

so childish. And she was growing into a woman. Or at least that's how she wanted Trey to see her.

"Whoops, my bad," Mia said, taking them. "Thanks."

"No problem." He shuffled awkwardly from foot to foot. "So, it was really awesome, the way you took charge back there, Helicity."

"Oh," she mumbled. "Thanks."

"You wouldn't want to hang out sometime, would you?" Trey suddenly blurted. "Not like a—a date or anything," he added hurriedly. "You, too, Mia."

Mia's lips twitched as if she was trying to suppress a smile. "Why not? We're staying up there, at the Beachside. And we're free tomorrow. So, if it's okay with Helicity . . ." She raised her eyebrows questioningly.

"I—um—yeah," Helicity stammered, the heat in her cheeks now rivaling that from the sun.

Trey broke into a wide grin and backpedaled the way he'd come. "Beachside. Tomorrow. See you then!"

The girls crouched to retrieve their flip-flops. "So. He seemed nice," Helicity commented casually.

"Definitely." Mia bumped her shoulder. "Also, he's into you."

"What? No, he's not!"

"Uh, yeah, he is! Which is why I left the buckets behind. Had to give him a reason to come after us. Or you, rather." Mia held up her hands. "Don't get me wrong. He's cute, but so not my type."

"What is your type?" Helicity wondered.

"Gingers with British accents. You know, the whole Ed Sheeran–Prince Harry–Ronald Weasley package. But do you ever see gorgeous redheaded guys on the beach? No. Because sunburn." Mia heaved a woebegone sigh.

Just then, the Y-shaped crosspiece on Helicity's flip-flop popped loose. As she knelt to fix it, Mia started tossing out ideas for the next day. "We could do the ferry again. Or head to North Jetty. Or— Huh. That's weird."

"What's weird?"

"Someone's waving to us from the Beachside deck."

Helicity straightened and shaded her eyes. The setting sun cast the person in silhouette, making it impossible for her to see his face. Then he shouted.

"Helicity! Mia! Hey!"

Helicity's jaw dropped. *"Andy?"*

"Hey, Hel!" her brother called. "Surprise!"

CHAPTER FIVE

"**H**ang on! I'll be right down!"

Andy didn't need to tell her to wait. Helicity was so stunned she couldn't have moved if she tried.

"What . . . when . . . how—?" she sputtered when he reached the path. Then she gave up on talking and simply hurled herself into her brother's arms.

After a moment, she wrinkled her nose and pulled away. "Um, no offense, but you kind of smell."

"Kind of?" Mia waved her hand through the air. An only child, she'd always viewed Andy as her own big brother—and she treated him with all the sarcastic disrespect of a bratty little sister. "That's the understatement of the century."

Andy laughed. "Well, I've been driving for two days straight, subsisting on nasty road food and sleeping in the car, so I'm not surprised. But let me put you both out of your misery."

Without missing a beat, he pulled off his T-shirt and ran into the waves. A pair of teenage girls walking nearby paused to watch him. Such admiring looks were nothing new. With his thick, wavy brown hair, sea-green eyes, and tall, athletic physique, Andy was undeniably good-looking. But it was his kindness and affability that made Helicity proud to call him her brother.

He dove under and splashed around, making a show of dousing his armpits with water and scrubbing his hair with his fingers. "Come on in!" he yelled.

"Why, so you can dunk me like you always do?" Mia yelled back. "Nice try, but no thanks!"

Helicity smiled broadly but kept her feet firmly onshore, too.

Her smile faded when Andy waded out. He looked worn-out, with dark circles under his eyes and hollows in his cheeks. His right arm moved with an awkward stiffness. It was badly shattered when the tornado flipped his car, and Andy had needed surgical implants—metal plates and screws—to repair the damage. The angry red scars were the only evidence of what lurked beneath his skin.

He saw where she was looking. His expression darkened. "Come on, Hel." He snatched up his shirt. "You've seen my scars before."

She lowered her gaze. "Sorry."

For a long moment, tension hung thick in the air between them. Then Mia intervened. "Well, I haven't seen them. So, I'm going to go ahead and take a good long look."

She stuck her hands on her hips and stared pointedly at his right arm. He growled and tried to catch her in a headlock. She skipped away to the path, laughing. Helicity and Andy followed, the sudden friction evaporating like the salty seawater on his skin.

"All right, now that you're less smelly," Helicity said, "tell me what you're doing here. And how you got here!"

"All will be revealed in good time," Andy said

evasively. "But right now, I'd love to get changed out of these filthy wet shorts and into some filthy dry shorts. Suze said I could use the outside shower."

"You met Suze?"

"She told me where to find you. Invited me to stay for dinner, too."

While Andy showered, Helicity ran up to their room to change into shorts and a tank top. She reached for Lana's necklace but then decided against wearing it. Andy knew the story behind it. It wasn't a story he liked to be reminded of. So she left the necklace on her nightstand.

Downstairs, Helicity found Andy dressed in fresh clothes and sitting in an Adirondack chair on the deck. "I could get used to this," he said, leaning his head back and closing his eyes against the late afternoon sunshine. "I think I'll take a little snooze."

Helicity thought he might, too, until his knee started jittering up and down like a mini jackhammer. "Whoa, bro. Just how much caffeine is running through your system right now?"

She took a seat next to him, nudging his bouncing knee with her foot until it stilled. "I'm really glad you're here, Andy. But . . . *why* are you here?"

He grimaced and opened his eyes. "Things at home are not good, Hel. Dad's on my case every hour of every day. 'Go to therapy. Get strong. Michigan State might still honor your scholarship if you get your arm back in working order.'" He gave a mirthless laugh. "Please. That door hasn't just closed, it's slammed in my face."

"But why would Dad keep on about it if it wasn't a possibility?" Helicity wondered. "I mean, your surgery was a success. And if you've been doing PT—"

"Are you seriously taking his side against me?"

Andy's anger flared so sudden and hot, Helicity shrank back. Like any brother and sister, they'd had their share of arguments. But she couldn't remember him ever lashing out at her that quickly and for something she felt didn't merit such a curt response.

"You have no idea what it's been like for me." Andy rocked up out of his chair and began pacing like a caged animal. "The constant nagging from Dad. The pitying looks from the people in town. Friends who are mysteriously unavailable all of a sudden. And *Mom*." He rolled his eyes. "Mom keeps trying to play peacemaker between Dad and me. Well, good luck with that. And don't get me started on physical therapy. More like physical *torture*. The stuff that PT guy made me do was worse than the accident and the surgery combined."

The fight seemed to leave him then. He sank back down into his chair and raked his fingers through his damp hair. It stood on end, making him look slightly deranged. "Every PT session was agony, Hel. So I quit. Dad thought I was still going, but I just drove around for the hour. I swear, if it weren't for—"

He abruptly stopped talking.

"Weren't for what?" Helicity prodded.

He flashed her a half smile. "For you. You're the only one who treated me the same after the accident. So, two days ago, I decided to come see you. My head was going to explode if I didn't leave, Hel, I swear. Like, *boom!*" He flared his fingers out from his temples to punctuate the explosion, then dropped his hands in his lap. "And so here I am. End of story."

It might have been the end of the story, but Helicity guessed it wasn't the *full* story. Andy was hiding something from her.

"Wait. Mom and Dad—they do know where you are, right?" she asked, suddenly alarmed.

"Well, I didn't exactly plan my itinerary with them, but yeah. I let them know where I was going. And that I got here."

"But *how* did you get here?" she persisted.

He avoided her eyes. "I got a ride."

Helicity was about to ask who with when she heard a car pull up. The engine growled like that of an older-model automobile before it cut out. A door slammed. Andy's eyes flicked toward the sound, then back to her.

"Wait," she said. "Is that your ride?"

He lifted his shoulders and let them fall. Frowning, she got up and looked over the deck railing. And suddenly, she knew why Andy had been so evasive.

A beat-up baby-blue sedan had pulled in next to the beach-mobile. The trunk was open, and the driver was leaning far inside, pawing through the contents. She couldn't see his face. But she didn't need to. She knew exactly who it was.

CHAPTER SIX

"**S**am."

Helicity rounded on Andy. "You came here with Sam."

Down below, the trunk closed with a hollow thump. Helicity tensed, her fingernails digging into her palms.

After Sam vanished from the hospital, she'd told herself that she didn't care if she ever saw him again. That any warm feelings she had for him had been replaced by cold indifference.

But her quickening breath and racing heart said otherwise.

As Sam's footsteps sounded on the stairs, her emotions bubbled in a hot, jumbled mess. Fury and hurt mixed with anticipation. She wanted to run inside, but she couldn't make her legs work.

And then Sam was there. He saw her and froze. The familiar zinging jolt of electricity struck her when their eyes met. So intense, it threatened to consume her. She dropped her gaze, breaking the connection. But just long enough to slow her breathing. To scold her heart for betraying her. Only when she was in control did she dare look at him again.

At first glance, he seemed the same—spiky black hair, ice-blue eyes, tall, thin build. His black leather jacket was missing, but he wore one of his favorite retro concert T-shirts with his jeans and black boots.

But there were differences, she now saw. A jagged scar, redder and more raw than Andy's, marred his forehead. His face was drawn, and his eyes, once filled with mischief and laughter, had a haunted look.

She recognized that look. She saw it every day when she gazed in the mirror.

"Fourteen."

Helicity's breath caught in her throat at hearing his

special nickname for her. He'd given it to her when they'd first met, after she insisted she was almost fourteen years old.

Andy moved to her side. "He came to the house a few days after you left for Texas," he said quietly. "Said he had to talk to you."

"And tell me what?" She directed her question at Andy. It was easier that way.

But Sam was the one who replied. "That I'm sorry. And to explain why I left."

Helicity lifted her chin and faced him. "So, tell me."

Sam looked miserable. "Guilt. After the accident . . . after what almost happened to you and Lana—I couldn't face you. So, when an opportunity to disappear came my way, I took it." He made a sound like a cross between a laugh and a sigh. "Turns out, leaving just made the guilt worse."

"You think he looks bad now? You should have seen him when he showed up on our doorstep," Andy joked.

Helicity shot her brother a look. He held up his hands in surrender and retreated into the house, mumbling about checking on his laundry.

Sam watched him go, then turned back to Helicity.

"Everything that happened that day was my fault. I convinced you to get in Lana's SUV to chase down that possible tornado. I drove too fast. I lost control on the bridge." His face contorted with anguish. "And I left you stranded in the river on top of the SUV and let those other storm chasers rescue me first. If you hadn't made it to shore in time, if you'd been swept away, too—"

His voice hitched. "Lana is in a coma because of choices I made that day. Selfish, stupid choices." He sat down in the chair Andy had vacated.

Helicity stared at him. Then she sat down, too. "You're right. Your choices were selfish and stupid." She paused. "But so were mine."

Sam started to protest, but she cut him off. "I knew going after the tornado was stupid. I could have— should have—tried harder to stop you. Instead, I pulled up the GPS on my phone and gave you directions! I led us straight into danger. So I'm as much to blame as you are for what happened to Lana. And believe me, I feel just as guilty."

They sat in silence. Then Sam said, "Did you ever go see her?"

Helicity reached for the lightning bolt necklace

before remembering it was still on her bedside table. "I visited her a few times before I came here."

Sam put his head in his hands. "I only went once. That was all I could take."

Helicity remembered how gutted she'd been at seeing Lana in the hospital. Yet unlike Sam, she'd gone back. She had owed Lana that much. "I guess we dealt with our guilt differently."

"Yeah." Sam raised his head. "I think maybe your way was better." He gave her a hesitant smile.

That smile unknotted something inside her. It wasn't just its tentativeness, though that was worlds apart from Sam's usual brash confidence. His smile seemed to be seeking her forgiveness even more than his words had. Seeing it, she felt the anger and hurt she'd been carrying since his disappearance ease. In its place was a bud of renewed trust.

So, she smiled back. "We should make a pact. No more stupid or selfish choices. Deal?"

Relief eased the tension in Sam's face. "Deal." He stuck out his hand.

When their palms clasped, Helicity experienced the same magnetic force she'd felt when she first saw him. His eyes widened slightly, and she wondered if he felt it, too.

Don't go there, she cautioned herself, dropping his hand and standing up to go inside.

"Fourteen?"

She fixed a smile on her face and pivoted back. "Hey, about that nickname. My birthday's in a few days. So, it's time to stop calling me Fourteen."

"Or," Sam countered with a hint of his old mischief, "I could start calling you Fifteen."

The deck door opened then. "Yo! Dinner!" Mia called.

While Helicity and Sam were outside, Mia had filled Suze in on the stranded dolphin. "I know where the marine mammal rehab center is," Suze informed them. "You can schedule a visit to the center. Although," she added, "I'm not sure you'd be able to see your dolphin right away."

Mia switched subjects from the dolphin to Trey. "He's super cute and really nice and totally into Helicity."

"Mia," Helicity chided, embarrassed as much by her comment as by the pointed way she directed it at Sam. He raised his eyebrows but said nothing.

Andy came out of the kitchen armed with their food—a huge bowl of pasta, another with salad, and a plate of warm crusty French bread. Suze followed closely behind. His gaze darted back and forth between Helicity and Sam questioningly.

Helicity sat down next to Mia. "We're good," she said simply.

Andy broke into a broad smile. "Awesome. Because Suze says we can stay here for the night, and it would have been awkward if you guys were still mad at each other."

"You didn't have to do that, Suze," Helicity said gratefully.

She waved away her thanks. "The rooms are available, they're friends and family, and there's supposed to be a thunderstorm tonight. No-brainer."

"Wait," Mia interjected. "If there hadn't been room here, what would you guys have done?"

"Camped out somewhere, probably," Andy replied as he helped himself to a small portion of pasta. "Sam's got a trunkload of gear—tents, sleeping bags, propane cookstove, you name it."

"I've been camping out a lot lately," Sam added vaguely.

Helicity's curiosity was piqued, but she didn't give in to it. What Sam did was none of her business . . . unless he wanted it to be.

"After tonight, though, then what?" Mia prodded. "Are you heading back to Michigan?"

Sam and Andy exchanged glances.

"Actually," Andy said, laying down his fork, "we were thinking of hanging around here for a while. Not *here* here," he added quickly when Suze cocked an eyebrow. "Like I said, we'll camp out. Pick up an odd job, maybe. I don't know about Sam, but I'm a little thin in the wallet department right now."

Sam made an "I'm good" gesture. Andy grinned at Helicity. "But you haven't heard the best part. When you're ready to head home, we'll all drive back together."

Helicity blinked in surprise. She'd come to Texas on a one-way ticket with no definite return date other than before the start of the school year. Driving back with Andy and Sam instead of flying with a chaperone— and maybe through turbulence—that appealed to her.

Suze, meanwhile, had latched on to Andy's quest for cash. "Odd jobs, huh? I know a friend of a friend who needs some house painting done. I'll hook you up with him, if you like."

"That'd be awesome."

After the meal, Suze shooed them to the fire pit. "Go on, have fun. Better hurry, though. The thunderstorm is due in a few hours."

Andy let out a big yawn and stood up. "Sorry, guys, but I'm going to skip the campfire."

Helicity's face fell with disappointment. "Really?"

"Sorry, Hel. The road trip is catching up with me. I gotta crash." Andy disappeared into his guest room.

Down at the fire pit, Sam got a blaze going. Orange-yellow sparks shot into the air, competing with the stars and the moon for brightest objects in the sky.

Mia pulled her chair close to Helicity. "So. You *really* okay with him being here?" She indicated Sam with a skeptical nod.

Helicity watched another spark shower vanish into the darkness. She wondered again why Sam had been camping for the past weeks. Where he'd gone. If he'd been alone . . . or with someone.

She suddenly realized Sam was staring intently at her through the flames. So intently, in fact, that she was afraid she'd spoken that last thought out loud. "Sam, I—"

"You look older," he interrupted with a slight frown.

"I . . . do?"

Beside her, Mia nodded. "He's right. It's your new hairstyle, I think. Makes you look more mature."

Helicity's hand crept to her hair. A week in the sea-soaked sunshine had warmed the sandy-brown locks to a lighter blond. Her skin had burnished to a golden tan, too. The changes made the green of her eyes stand out, she'd noticed in the mirror that morning.

Sam tilted his head. "It could be your hair, I guess. Seems like something more than that, though." He got up to fetch more wood.

Helicity hugged her knees closer to her chest. "You know what, Mia? I think everything with Sam is going to be fine."

CHAPTER SEVEN

B *oom!*

    Helicity and Mia sat straight up in their beds.

"Holy moly!" Mia's wide eyes gleamed in the darkness. "I felt that in my gut!"

"Me too."

Helicity, Mia, and Sam had hung around the campfire for more than an hour. Helicity had peppered Sam with questions about the road trip—whose idea it had been, where they ate and slept, and what they talked about.

"The trip just sort of happened," Sam confessed. "I

said I wished I could see you in person. Next thing I knew, your brother had packed a bag. We ate wherever, took turns driving and sleeping."

He poked the fire with a stick. "I thought he'd ask me about . . . well, you know. About what happened. Or yell at me. Blame me for putting you in danger. I think some part of me wanted him to." He sat back. "But he never did. Mostly, if he wasn't sleeping, he just stuck in his earbuds and zoned out."

Helicity would have liked to ask more. But it was getting late, and a bank of clouds was rolling in. So they doused the fire and called it a night.

The boom of thunder that woke her and Mia announced that those clouds had grown into full-blown thunderstorms.

It was the first storm Helicity had experienced since the flash flood. There'd been a few overcast days in Michigan, and in Texas, the weather had been consistently hot, humid, and sunny. She'd been grateful for the calm but wondered how she'd feel when the weather turned foul, as it inevitably would. Uneasy? Fearful? Runaway panic?

The thunder awakened a reaction just as powerful:

longing. Despite the tragedies the weather had thrust upon her, she still felt its pull. She let that longing tug her forward now.

"Where are you going?" Mia whispered hoarsely when Helicity threw back the covers.

"To watch the storm. You want to come?"

Another thunderclap sent Mia diving beneath the covers. "No thanks. I'm good here," came her muffled reply.

Helicity stepped onto the landing, closing the door quietly behind her. Across from the half wall, the picture windows framed the sea and sky. The storm played out in front of her like a movie on the silver screen.

More than anything, she wanted to be in that movie. But going outside during a thunderstorm was beyond dangerous. Lightning was predictably unpredictable, striking in the blink of an eye. So, she leaned her elbows on the wall to watch from the safety of the beach house.

The storm unfolded with breathtaking fury. Billowing clouds crowded the beach. The usually glassy-calm sea was wind-whipped and crawled higher onto the

shore, biting chunks out of the sand. A bolt of lightning zigzagged from the clouds, illuminating the vast
Gulf of Mexico. The next bolt branched across the
sky. That was cloud-to-cloud lightning—meaning the
storm was mature, losing some of its power, and probably beginning to die.

Dying or not, the lightning's white-hot bril-
liance temporarily blinded her. She blinked to clear
her vision, listening with awe as a crackle of thunder exploded into another bone-rattling *boom* before
grumbling away into silence. A light patter of fat
raindrops rapped at the windows and roof like
curious fingers, then quickly escalated to a thrumming drumbeat.

One part of Helicity's brain drank in the pure wonder of the sights and sounds. Another mulled over
how the storm likely developed. Thunderstorms, she
knew, were born from instability in the troposphere—
the layer of the atmosphere closest to the earth—and
the convergence of hot air, cold air, and water vapor.
It had been hotter than usual that afternoon. As the
land heated up, the hot air above it had risen higher
and met a cooler, vapor-laden air mass coming in from

the sea. After that meeting, it was just a matter of time before the thunderstorm formed.

The sky lit up with another lightning flash. Helicity counted off a few beats, then mimicked Andy's flared finger explosion in time with the thunderclap.

The boom ended with another long, low rumble. In the silence that followed, she heard a downstairs door open and close. Footsteps on the tiled floors tapped out a counterpoint to the rain. Then another door opened and closed.

That was the kitchen door, she realized. *But who would be going outside in this weather?*

She knew the answer before she even finished asking herself the question.

Sam.

Like her, he would have been drawn out of bed to witness the storm. But unlike her, he had decided to experience it firsthand.

A stupid choice, she thought, remembering their pact. Maybe he'd been joking when he'd made it. But she hadn't been.

She raced silently down the stairs and skidded around the corner into the kitchen. She got to the door just in time to see Sam's sedan pulling out of the parking area.

A bitter taste rose in her mouth.

One night. He couldn't even keep his promise for one night.

The brief reprieve, the warm feelings for Sam that had crept back in, were again replaced by . . . not indifference, but frosty anger. Anger over the chances he was taking with his safety. Anger over the ease with which he'd tossed aside her trust. Anger with herself for still yearning for him despite it all.

Outside the picture windows, the storm raged on. She tried to recapture the exhilaration she'd felt just moments before. But Sam's broken promise had ruined the thunderstorm's terrible beauty for her. She turned away and went back to bed.

The next morning, Helicity awoke later than usual. To her surprise, Trey was there already, seated at the kitchen island across from Mia. He greeted her with a broad smile that lit up his handsome face. He smelled good, too. Like clean laundry and vanilla.

"Helicity! Thank God!" He wiggled a thumb at Mia. "She's been giving me the third degree since I got here."

"I'm just trying to get to know you," Mia protested.

Helicity smiled. "So, what have you learned?"

Mia ticked off her fingers. "That he's fifteen, his parents have a cabin on a lake, and his real name is Ferdinand Eugenio Valdez . . . the Third."

He groaned. "Now you know why I go by *Trey*."

"I don't know." Mia tapped a finger to her chin. "I think Ferdinand suits you. Or maybe just Ferd?"

Trey groaned again. They were all cracking up when Sam walked in from the deck.

"I could hear you guys laughing from outside. What's so funny?"

At the campfire, Helicity had invited Sam to join them on their adventure, earning her a frown from Mia. She'd ignored it. Now, stung by Sam's broken promise, she ignored him instead.

Oblivious, Sam followed her to the refrigerator. "I've been down to the beach already. The storm blew in some seriously weird stuff. And how 'bout that storm? Pretty impressive, huh?"

The open refrigerator breathed cool air on Helicity's

face, but that didn't prevent her blood from starting to boil. "You'd know better than me about how impressive it was."

Sam caught her tone. "Everything all right?"

She slammed the door and glared at him. "I saw you go out in the storm last night, Sam."

She expected him to protest his innocence. But he just looked puzzled. "You're right, I was outside. I got some great video and photos, in fact. But I don't get why that would make you mad."

"You don't— Are you *kidding* me?"

Helicity was so affronted that her voice rose a notch. Mia jumped off her seat to stand next to her. "What did he do this time, Hel?" she asked, darting daggers at Sam.

"Nothing!" Sam said.

"'Nothing.' Seriously?" Helicity stabbed a finger at him. "Yesterday afternoon, we made a promise not to make stupid choices. Last night, you broke that promise. Took off in your car while the thunderstorm was in full force."

"Whoa, wait, what?" Sam held up his hands. "No, I didn't."

Helicity's jaw dropped. "You just admitted you did!"

"I said I was *outside*," Sam corrected. "Which I was. I watched the storm from under the deck."

Helicity narrowed her eyes. "Yeah, right."

"Wait. I can prove it." He disappeared into his room and returned with a minuscule but expensive-looking video camera. He'd had a similar device attached to his car's dashboard, to record storms he pursued by himself, Helicity remembered. This camera appeared to be brand-new.

"Look." Sam positioned the camera on the kitchen island where they could all see the tiny digital screen and hit PLAY.

The video started off with the large boom of thunder that had awoken Helicity and Mia. Sam must have been up already, though, for the images were clearly taken from outside the house. Just as clearly, the video had been shot from beneath the deck. Glimpses of the fire pit, the house's support posts, and the outside shower revealed as much. And Sam's voice came through loud and clear. Unless he could be in two places at one time, he hadn't been the one in the car last night.

Helicity stared at the granite countertop with a mixture of relief and shame. "I owe you an apology. I'm sorry I didn't believe you."

"Yeah. I'm sorry you didn't, either." He let out a big sigh. "But I get it."

Mia spoke up then. "If you didn't take your car, who did?"

"It must have been Andy. I gave him the spare key on our trip down here."

"Wait," Helicity said. "Where *is* Andy?"

The others looked at one another and shrugged. "I've been up since eight, and I haven't seen him," Mia said.

Helicity's heart skipped a beat. Andy prided himself on being an early riser. During football season, he would get up before dawn to lift weights or take a run before school. He'd fallen out of the habit after the accident but was still up and about by nine.

It was now ten thirty.

"Oh, my God." She met Sam's eyes. "He didn't make it back!"

CHAPTER EIGHT

Helicity's heart was in her throat as she and Sam ran to the kitchen door. She started breathing again when she saw Sam's sedan next to the beach-mobile in the parking area. "He's here." She rested her head against the door's glass.

"Who's here?"

Helicity wheeled around to see Andy, still in his sleep T-shirt and shorts, wandering into the kitchen. "You! *You're* here!"

Andy yawned sleepily. "'Course I am. Where else would I be?"

"I saw you drive off last night. Where did you go?"

"Last night?" Andy glanced at Sam and the others, then back to Helicity. "I got hungry," he said defensively. "I didn't feel right helping myself to Suze's food. So, I borrowed Sam's car and— He gave me a key, did he tell you that?"

Helicity nodded impatiently. "And?"

"And I drove around to find something to eat. Turns out the only thing open was an all-night convenience store. So, I bought some snacks and came back. I can show you the receipt if you don't believe me." He shook his head, then went to the sink and filled a glass with water, which he drank in one go.

Helicity trailed after him. "Andy, going out like that was a really bad idea."

Andy smirked. "What, you think I was going to get struck by lightning or something?"

"Actually," Trey volunteered, "I heard a big ol' tree got zotted in the storm. It was on another part of the peninsula, but still."

Andy frowned. "Who are you?"

"This is Ferdinand," Mia said, "and he wants a tour of the Beachside."

"It's *Trey*, and I do?" Trey asked. Mia gave him a

significant look. "I mean, I do!" he amended hurriedly. Trey looked uneasy as he begrudgingly followed Mia out of the kitchen, stealing one last look at Helicity. She could feel his eyes on her. She could feel Sam's eyes, too.

Sam waited until they were gone, then turned to Andy. "Helicity is right. Going out last night wasn't smart, not with that lightning, the rain, and the wind. Plus, it was dark, and you don't know the area." He shook his head. "Could have been bad, man."

Andy tilted his glass at Sam. "Key phrase there? Could have been." He waved a hand at himself. "As you can see, I'm totally fine."

"But I didn't know that," Helicity murmured. "When no one had seen you this morning, I thought . . ." She bit her lip to stop it from trembling.

Andy had worn a sarcastic look up until then. Now his expression softened. "Listen, Hel. I'm sorry. I didn't mean to scare you. But I'm a big boy. I can take care of myself."

Helicity nodded. "I know that. Just do me a favor, though, okay?"

"Name it."

"Don't get hungry in the middle of the night again."

He laughed. "I'll do my best." He refilled his glass, drained it, and put it on the island. "Nice equipment," he commented, tapping the video camera. "Bet that set you back a few pesos."

Sam shrugged like it was no big deal.

"Speaking of pesos," Andy added, picking up Helicity and Mia's tip jar from its spot near to the sink, "your earnings are adding up. I might have to ask for a handout if this painting job doesn't work out." He set down the jar with a laugh. "Now, have you seen Suze? She offered to take me to meet with the guy who needs the painting done."

Andy and Suze took off in the beach-mobile a short while later. Mia and Trey, meanwhile, had come up with a plan for the day—a trip to a Galveston amusement park.

"Mia says you've never been to one before," Trey said, pretending to be aghast.

"You haven't?" Sam looked surprised.

Helicity shrugged. "Not unless you count those traveling carnivals."

"Which I don't," Trey said. "So, the amusement park it is!"

A short while later, they were on the ferry to Galveston, Sam's car tucked neatly among other vehicles on the deck. Helicity hurried to the bow of the boat, hoping to see dolphins again. After she climbed the stairs and found the perfect viewing spot, she tugged at her shorter locks, in an attempt to keep the hair out of her face. Sam joined her, and suddenly, she flashed back to their first—and last—ferry ride together.

Sam seemed to read her mind. "Hard to believe that less than a month ago, we were headed across Lake Michigan for the start of our storm-chasing summer," he murmured.

"You went belowdecks to check out Mo West with Ray," she recalled with a wistful smile.

"Pretty sure I drove him nuts with all my questions."

"No," Helicity disagreed. "He might have complained about you, but I know he liked you."

"Thanks." Sam kept his eyes on the waves. "I wonder if he still does."

"You haven't talked to him?"

Sam shook his head. "How can I, Fourteen? His best friend is in a coma because of me. If our roles were reversed, and something he did hurt someone I cared about"—he glanced sideways at Helicity, holding her gaze so that her cheeks grew warm—"I wouldn't want to talk to him, either."

He pushed off from the railing and walked away, leaving Helicity to watch for dolphins by herself. She wished he had stayed.

The amusement park was located on a pier that jutted into the Gulf of Mexico. There were rides of all kinds—a roller coaster, a Ferris wheel, a flume boat with a sign that gleefully promised YOU WILL GET WET! They wandered about before stopping next to a giant pendulum ringed with outward-facing seats that hurtled through the air while spinning in dizzying circles. Its riders were screaming. With excitement or terror, Helicity wasn't sure.

Trey pointed at the pendulum. "We should do that first."

Mia nodded enthusiastically. "Absolutely!"

"I'm up for it," Sam agreed. "What about you, Fourteen?"

Helicity wasn't so sure. The pendulum sparked an

uneasiness deep inside her. The crazy spinning. The dirt and debris it kicked up when it swept over the ground. And the screaming. The constant screaming. It was nothing like the real-life tornado she'd survived. And yet she'd broken out in cold sweat just looking at it.

But she didn't want to spoil the fun, so she swallowed her trepidation and nodded. "Yeah. Let's do it."

On their way over to the ride, Trey asked, "Sam, why do you call Helicity Fourteen?"

Sam looked at him as if it was obvious, then shrugged and told him the story. "The nickname stuck," he finished, "though there were plenty of times when Hel—with two *L*'s, that is—seemed to fit her better!"

Trey glanced at her, clearly nonplussed at Sam's dig at her expense. Helicity smiled to reassure him she didn't take it the wrong way. At the same time, she noted how different his manners were from Sam's. He would never use sarcasm to address a lady, not with his gracious southern style.

Fifteen minutes later, they were strapped into chairs. Feet dangling, Helicity felt her uneasiness grow.

A bored attendant went over the safety regulations. "This is your last chance to disembark this gravity-defying thrill ride," he finished in a prerecorded-sounding monotone. "So, raise your hand if you've changed your mind."

I should get off, Helicity thought desperately. But she couldn't unclench her hands from the armrests to signal the attendant.

Sam grinned at her, then did a double take. "You okay there, Fourteen?" When she didn't answer, he started to call for the attendant. But he was too late.

Without another warning, the pendulum swooped forward. Helicity gasped as her feet flew out into nothingness. Sky rushed toward her. Then ground, then sky again, everything whipping past faster and faster as the chairs whirled and swung, whirled and swung. Her vision swam. She squeezed her eyes shut to block out the blur. But that didn't stop the panic from rising within her.

Beside her, Mia shrieked—not in terror, but in exhilaration. "This is *awesome!*"

"Wooo-hooo!" Trey responded.

Helicity's throat was so tight, she couldn't make a

sound. Then, on the next downward swoop, she felt something bump against her chest.

Lana's necklace.

Helicity had automatically put it on that morning. Since the plane, she'd worn it tucked beneath her shirt so she could feel its reassuring touch against her skin. But it must have come free, for now, like her feet, the lightning bolt was flying out and back.

Grab it.

The thought came to her in a flash. Holding the necklace on the plane had given her something real, something solid to focus on. But this time, she couldn't bring herself to let go of the pendulum's handholds. So instead, she latched on to the image of the lightning bolt. At the same time, she silently repeated her mantra.

I'm a survivor, not a victim. A survivor. Not. A. VICTIM.

The pendulum swept back down again as that last word pounded in her mind. Helicity took a deep breath and opened her eyes.

And then she screamed and let herself enjoy the lack of control. She realized repeating her mantra gave her that bit of extra courage and she finally relaxed. Strangely, one of the most relaxing moments she had had in months came on a rickety ride at the amusement park.

CHAPTER NINE

"**O**h, my God." Trey held some papers in his hands. He looked from the top one to Helicity. "I am so sorry."

Mia swiped it from him, glanced at it, and then gave a snort of laughter. "Oh, man. Sorry, Hel. The camera caught you mid-scream. Not your best look."

At some point during the pendulum ride, an automated camera had snapped photos of the foursome. Mia, Helicity, and Sam didn't know that. Trey did. He'd sneaked off to the photo booth and returned with four copies. He looked perfect in the shot, staring directly into the camera and showing two thumbs up.

Trying not to laugh, he handed Helicity her copy.

She stared at herself for a long moment. Then she looked up at them, eyes shining. "I look ridiculous. But I don't care. I love this photo."

It was true. The photo had captured the exact moment she'd released her panic into the air with her scream. The ride had only lasted another minute after that, but she'd experienced it with her eyes wide open. And while her heart had hammered in her chest the whole time—and afterward while they waited for Trey to reappear—its beat had been fueled by triumphant elation, not panic.

Because I'm a survivor, she thought, gazing at the picture again. Allowing herself to bask in her own cheesiness.

Sam was studying his copy of the photo, too. Suddenly, his eyes widened. "Fourteen! Are you wearing Lana's necklace?"

After the ride, Helicity had tucked the necklace beneath her shirt. Now she pulled it out, holding the charm so the lightning bolt caught the sunlight. "Yes."

"Who's Lana, and why do you have her necklace?" Trey asked curiously.

Mia shot Helicity a concerned glance. "Hey, anybody else hungry?" she said, clearly trying to change the subject to save Helicity from dredging up disturbing memories. "I think I saw some candy apples for sale."

"It's okay, Mia," Helicity said. "I—I kind of feel like talking about it, if that's all right."

Mia sat beside her. "You sure?"

"Yeah. If Sam doesn't mind, that is."

He tightened his lips but nodded.

Helicity took a deep breath and told Trey everything. About the tornado and Andy. About meeting Lana and Sam and going on the storm-chasing expedition. About being caught by the flash flood and Lana coming in after her. "Her necklace came off in my hand when the waves pulled her away from me," she ended.

It was the first time she'd told anyone the whole story. She downplayed Sam's part—that was his story to tell, not hers—but was completely honest about her own role in Andy's and Lana's tragedies. To have been otherwise would have felt like a lie.

Yet she couldn't meet Trey's eyes. She wondered how her tale had sounded to him, an outsider untouched by and unconnected to any of it. Maybe Mia was right, and he was interested in her. But what did he think of her now that she'd revealed her terrible past?

Trey hadn't said a word while she was talking. Now he slowly sat down next to her. "Dang, girl," he murmured. "What you went through—what you both went through," he added with a nod at Sam, "must have been . . . I don't know." He shook his head. "Just *dang*." She saw understanding spread through Trey, then a look of unease as he processed how tight Sam and Helicity must be after sharing such a dramatic past.

Mia slipped her arm around Helicity and gave her a squeeze. "Dang is right," she whispered, cutting an appreciative look at Trey.

Sam had been quiet, too. Now he broke his silence. "Fourteen. Before the ride started . . . before you screamed, you weren't okay, were you?"

"No." Helicity hesitated, then told him how repeating her mantra and visualizing the lightning bolt had brought her panic under control. "And I'll tell you something else, too."

"What's that?"

"I thought I needed to wear this to feel in control. But that's not true." She traced her finger over the lightning bolt's jagged edge. "I just need to keep it safe so when Lana wakes up, I can hand it back to her."

Sam gave the bolt a gentle tap. "Here's hoping that happens really soon."

After a few hours in the amusement park, the foursome had had enough of thrill rides and crowds. Trey led the way to a nearby beach. They walked along a stretch of the stone seawall that ran parallel to the Gulf. Finally, Mia declared herself too weary to take another step. She plunked down in the sand with her back against the wall and immediately dozed off. Helicity was envious of her friend and wished she, too, could sleep with such peacefulness. Sam wandered off toward a nearby jetty that stretched out into the Gulf.

Trey watched him go, then motioned to Helicity. "There's a statue I think you'll like a little farther on. Want to see it?"

Curious, she fell into step beside him. "So what is this— Oh!"

The statue was just past a grove of palm trees. Cast in dark bronze, it showed a pair of dolphins standing on their tails—a mother and baby judging by their size and the way the smaller one was nestled close to the bigger one.

"It's so sweet." Helicity climbed onto the statue's stone pedestal and stroked the mother dolphin's back. The bronze was warm and rough under her fingertips.

Trey joined her. "I wanted to take you to the marine mammal rehab facility to see your dolphin today. It's just a few blocks from here. But they told me that we'd need an appointment." He gestured to the statue. "This was the best I could do, dolphin-wise."

Trey's thoughtfulness touched Helicity, and she smiled.

"Hold that!" He whipped out his phone, leaned in close, and took a selfie of them with the statue.

Helicity blinked when she saw the photo. Tendrils of her sun-kissed hair had mingled with his curls. Her eyes, startlingly green against her tanned skin, were crinkled at the corners from her smile. Trey was smiling, too. But not at the camera. At her.

We look like a couple. The thought crossed her mind

before she could stop it. *And we look good together. Like we are supposed to be together.* Momentarily disconcerted, she moved away to the other side of the statue and pretended to be fascinated by the smaller dolphin.

You only met him yesterday, she scolded herself. *For all you know, he's a total creep.*

Somehow, though, she knew he wasn't. His shyness on the beach the day before, his eagerness to share the statue with her, and the happiness shining through his smile in the photo—everything about Trey sent a glow of warmth through her. She liked the feeling. She liked *him.* Equally important, she trusted him.

Just then, a gust of wind carried a distant shout to her ear. She shaded her eyes and spotted Sam standing alone at the tip of the jetty. A wave broke against the boulders, sending up a blast of saltwater spray. Others might have ducked to avoid getting wet, but Sam flung his arms wide and yelled again, as if daring the ocean to bring on its worst.

His wild fury sparked something inside her—it was that longing again. It knocked up against the warmth Trey had spread through her, demanding attention. Suddenly confused and feeling tornadic, she jumped off the statue's pedestal and started walking back toward Mia.

Trey trotted after her. "Helicity? You okay?"

She gave a quick smile. "Yeah. But it's getting late. And you are too cute. So, it's time to go." She wanted Trey to know she was interested, too. And she wanted most of all to push herself further from Sam.

CHAPTER TEN

"Still no dolphins?"

At Trey's question, Helicity straightened up from the ferry railing and shook her head. Once again, she'd wandered to the bow after they boarded, claiming she wanted to watch for dolphins. But in truth, she wanted—needed—time alone to calm the emotional storm brewed up by Trey and Sam.

Not that it had helped. Those emotions were still roiling when the others came looking for her.

"So, check out that lighthouse." Trey pointed to a

tall, dark structure silhouetted against the horizon. It was such a prominent feature, Helicity was surprised she hadn't noticed it on her first return ferry trip a week earlier.

"Why is it black?" she asked, grateful to have something normal to focus on. "I thought all lighthouses were white."

"It used to be black-and-white striped," Trey replied. "The outside is covered with cast-iron plates that have completely rusted over the years. The weather turned the white stripes to black, and the black ones even blacker."

"Can we go inside it, see how it works?" Sam wanted to know.

Trey shook his head. "It's privately owned now, and anyway, it's not in great condition. The owners are trying to raise money to fix it up, but . . ." He shrugged.

"Suze told me a story about the lighthouse." Mia turned to Helicity and Sam. "You guys will like this. Apparently, like a hundred years ago, two hurricanes swept across Bolivar."

"A Cat-4 one hit on September 8, 1900," Helicity supplied. Her brow furrowed. "Six thousand people died."

"And there was another one in August of 1915," Sam added. "Both just about decimated Bolivar and Galveston."

Trey raised his eyebrows. "Wow. You guys really *are* weather junkies."

"You have no idea," Mia said with an elaborate eye roll. "Anyway, that lighthouse saved lives. Sixty people rode out the 1915 hurricane inside it. Twice that many in 1900."

Helicity stared at the black tower, trying to imagine more than a hundred people huddled inside as hurricane-force winds and driving rain pounded the exterior. "They must have been terrified." She knew what that felt like.

The ferry docked a few minutes later. As they drove off the boat, Helicity got a text from Andy.

> Got the painting job. Started today.
> Suze says we can stay 2nite.

Reading the text, she felt a stab of guilt. She'd been so caught up in her own emotional whirlwind, she hadn't given Andy a second thought all day. She texted him back.

> Beach walk when you get back? And let's call Mom and Dad.

Andy's reply was a cryptic.

> C U L8R

"L8R" turned out to be much later than Helicity expected. She was still waiting for Andy two hours after dinner. Mia was in their room, talking with her mother back in Michigan, and Sam was getting gas and purchasing the beach permit needed to camp out on Crystal Beach. Suze was out with friends.

To pass the time, Helicity wrote in her journal, spilling out her thoughts about what had happened at the amusement park and her jumbled feelings for Sam and Trey.

They are so totally different. Trey is like a lazy summer day—warm and relaxed and easygoing. And Sam? He's like a thunderstorm waiting to happen.

She'd just finished writing when Andy finally walked in. He had white paint smears on his T-shirt and shorts, and his hair was flecked with tiny white dots. His nose and forearms had a hint of sunburn.

He reminded Helicity of their father for some reason, though she couldn't figure out why at first.

It's his eyes, she decided with a pinch of concern. The dark circles made him look haggard. Their father had had those same circles after the tornado.

"Hey!" she said, getting to her feet. "I'm still up for that walk if you are."

He gave her a blank look.

"The walk on the beach. I texted you about it, remember?" she prompted.

Andy shook his head. "Sorry. I'm going to have to take a rain check." He moved past her toward his bedroom. "I have just enough time to grab a shower before Johnny comes back to get me."

Helicity blinked. "Johnny? Who's Johnny?"

"Another guy on the paint crew."

That, apparently, was the only information she was going to get. "Well, what about our call with Mom and Dad?"

Andy stiffened. "Like I said, I have to take a shower. Johnny will be here any minute. I don't have time for a phone call. Or any interest in listening to Dad."

He stalked off without another word, firmly closing

his bedroom door and leaving Helicity staring after him in consternation. A buzz from her phone broke the spell.

MOM AND DAD, the screen ID informed her. She swiped to answer the call.

"Hey, guys," she said with false brightness.

"Helicity! Darling!" her mother greeted. "How are you? Is Andy there, too?"

"No, sorry, you just have me tonight. Andy's . . . out."

"Oh." Her mother's disappointment came through loud and clear. "Well, let me put you on speakerphone so Dad can hear, too. There. Say hello, dear."

"Hello, dear." Her father's voice sounded tinny and distant.

"Ha, ha, Dad. How are things going up there? How's the new house coming?"

He blew out a long breath. "Slower than I'd like, but faster than others here. Town's still in a shambles. That tornado." He stopped talking, and Helicity could envision him shaking his head. "I swear, I'll never understand why you find those things so fascinating. They're terrible. Don't have to look any further than our own family to see that."

"Joe," Helicity's mother said wearily. "Not now."

Her father grunted. "Fine. Tell us about Andy, then."

"Yes," her mother agreed. "Is he . . . how is he?"

Helicity considered telling them that Andy seemed tired but changed her mind when she heard the concern in her mother's voice. Instead, she told them about his painting job.

"It was a huge surprise to have him show up here, I've got to say," she added. "I can't believe you guys didn't tell me he was coming!"

Her statement was met with silence. Then her father cleared his throat. "Pretty hard to tell something you have no knowledge of."

She frowned into the phone, puzzled. "What do you mean?"

"Oh, Helicity." Her mother's voice was tremulous. "Andy took off without telling us. We had no idea where he was until he texted us. By then, he was half-way to Texas."

Helicity was too dumbfounded to react. Luckily, a knock on the door saved her from having to. "Guys, I'm sorry, but there's someone at the door and I'm the only one here to answer it. We'll talk again another night when Andy's around, okay? Love you. Bye!"

She hung up before they could protest. She opened the kitchen door—and immediately wished she hadn't.

Standing in the shadows was a scruffy-looking teenage boy. His shaggy, unkempt blond hair matched a patchy growth of beard on his chin. A bad case of acne turned his face into a craggy red mess that was hard to look at. His T-shirt might have been white once but was now gray and dingy and, judging from the smell, badly in need of a wash. Skinny legs poked out of oversize, drooping shorts. He wore tattered flip-flops on his feet and a row of shark teeth on a leather cord around his neck.

Helicity had always tried to see the good in people. But when she saw him, her mind screamed one word: *dirtbag*.

"'S up," he drawled, jerking his chin at her. "Drew here?"

"Drew?" Even the boy's voice made her skin crawl. "I'm sorry, but you must have the wrong house. There's no Drew here."

She hoped he'd take the hint and leave. Instead, he

leaned against the doorjamb, his gaze roaming around Suze's kitchen. It paused briefly on Helicity and Mia's tip jar before returning to her. She took a step back and was about to call for Andy when her brother emerged from his room rubbing a towel over his damp hair.

"Johnny! My man!" he boomed.

Helicity's jaw dropped. *This* was who her brother was hanging out with instead of her?

Johnny shot Andy with a slow-motion finger gun, then whirled his hand with an impatient gesture. "Come on. Time to rock and roll."

Andy tossed the wet towel into his bedroom, pulled the door shut, and crossed into the kitchen. "See you later, Hel."

Hurt and confusion rooted Helicity to the spot. "Yeah. See you later . . . *Drew.*"

Andy paused in midstep. Then he reached over and flicked a finger through her short hair. "You know, Hel," he muttered, "you're not the only one who needed a change after everything that happened."

Then he was gone.

CHAPTER ELEVEN

Despite being exhausted from her long day, Helicity tossed and turned all night, wondering and worrying about Andy. In the morning, she rapped on his door, hoping to talk to him before he left for work. But her brother had already cleared out of his room. She'd have to wait until that afternoon, when he returned to set up the campsite on Crystal Beach.

If *he returns,* she groused to herself as she gathered up his dirty linens. *Maybe he'll get a better offer from Johnny.*

Andy did show up, but late, and in a foul mood.

Helicity didn't care. She'd been stewing all day, and now she wanted answers.

"Why didn't you tell Mom and Dad you were coming to see me?" she demanded as they carried gear from Sam's car to the beach.

Andy dumped his armload, then began pulling tent equipment from its sack. "Come on, Hel. You think they would have let me go if I had?" He thrust a pole through a tent sleeve.

"Okay, fine, that's fair," she admitted as she handed him another pole. "And I'm really glad you're here. Except . . ."

Andy gave her an impatient look as he slotted the rod into place. "Except what?"

"Except we haven't spent any time together since you got here!" she blurted. "And then when I thought we would last night, you went out with that Johnny guy instead."

"That Johnny guy," Andy echoed tightly, "offered to show me around the peninsula." He jerked his head at Trey, who was working with Sam and Mia on the other tent. "Or are you the only one allowed to make new friends here?"

"Of course not. But come on. Johnny's not exactly the type of person you usually hang out with."

"Really." Andy slipped the last pole in place and jammed it and the others into the sand. The tent popped up fully formed, its nylon sides ruffling in the light breeze. "Now you know how I felt when I first met Sam."

Helicity's eyes widened. "It's not the same, and you know it!"

"You're right, it's not. You and Sam being friends didn't make sense to me, not at first, but I trusted your judgment. Too bad you don't trust mine."

The truth of his accusation hit home. "I'm sorry. If you tell me Johnny's a good guy, then I'll believe you." She avoided his eyes when she apologized, though, because Andy always knew when she was lying. And she knew nothing he said would make her trust Johnny. Gut instinct refused to let her.

Instead of looking at him, she looked over at the other tent. Mia had her hand on Trey's arm, and they were laughing together. A flare of jealousy lit within her. She looked away, only to find Sam watching her. His ice-blue eyes locked onto her sea-green ones for a long moment—long enough for her to forget to breathe, for her heart to race as fast as a hummingbird's, for heat to flush her cheeks. The rush threatened to overwhelm her. She wrenched her gaze away. "I'll get the rest of the stuff."

She was digging in the trunk of Sam's car when she felt a hand on her shoulder. Startled, she whirled around to find Trey grinning at her.

"Sorry, didn't mean to scare you!" he said. "But Mia just told me that it's your birthday in two days. Why didn't you say something?"

Helicity handed him a sleeping bag and a battery-operated lamp. "I forgot, actually," she confessed. "There's just been so much going on."

"Well, the only thing that's going to be *going on* two nights from now is an amazing birthday party for you!"

Helicity protested that she didn't need a big celebration, but Trey wouldn't listen. "You won't have to do a thing except show up. Mia and I will do the rest." Then he paused. "Except for the cake. We'll get Suze to do that. But everything else"—he dropped a pretend grenade—"*boom!* Done!"

Trey was as good as his word. Two nights later, Helicity stood in the Beachside parking area with a bandanna covering her eyes, waiting for Mia to escort her to her party.

"Is this really necessary?" she growled, plucking at the fabric.

"Yes," Mia answered. "You know how I like a big reveal. Now, hold my arm."

Helicity sighed but did as she was told. Mia seemed to be leading her in crazy circles over hard-packed dirt, grass, and sand. When the sand deepened beneath her feet, she realized she'd moved onto the beach. Mia stopped her several steps later and whispered in her ear. "FYI, Trey did most of this himself. You ready?"

Helicity nodded.

Mia whipped off the blindfold. "Happy birthday!"

"Oh . . . wow!"

Helicity had been honest when she said she didn't need a big celebration. But now she was glad Trey hadn't listened. Mia, Sam, and Suze stood surrounded by a ring of lit tiki torches. In the middle of the blazing circle was a picnic table set with a white tablecloth. A bucket of sand with a single fat white candle served as the centerpiece. Scattered around the bucket was shiny dolphin-shaped confetti. The beach-mobile was parked nearby, playing pop music from a sound system someone had hooked up to its battery.

Trey stepped forward holding something behind his back. Helicity suspected it was a bouquet of flowers. She was wrong.

"Sparklers!" she crowed.

Grinning, Trey handed her a thin metal stick tipped with a small bulb of chemicals that, when ignited, would send up a shower of brilliant white sparks. He quickly passed out sparklers to Mia, Suze, and Sam.

"Wait," Helicity said. "Where's Andy?"

"Um, he's on his way," Mia replied. "Said to start without him."

Helicity's happiness dimmed, but only for a moment. Then Trey fired up a match and touched it to her sparkler. The tip sputtered to life.

"My turn!" Mia cried. Trey lit hers, and she grabbed Helicity's hand. "Remember what we used to do with these at Lake Michigan?"

"You know I do!"

Still holding hands, they sprinted toward the Gulf,

blazing sparklers held aloft. When they reached the water's edge, they stopped short. Their eyes met.

"I will if you will," Mia dared.

"Let's go!"

Hand in hand, they dashed fully clothed into the surf, splashing and whooping and flailing their sparklers through the air. The water reached their knees. They kept going. Up to their waists and deeper still. Then as one, they dove under, dousing their sparklers but reigniting something within themselves they'd lost.

They surfaced together, falling against each other and laughing so hard that tears sprang to their eyes and mingled with the salty water. Helicity hugged Mia tightly. "Thank you," she whispered. "For everything."

Mia touched her forehead to Helicity's. "That's what best friends are for." She grinned. "Now let's get out of here before a shark gets us."

As they raced out, Helicity saw that Sam had his video camera trained on them.

"Happy birthday . . . Fifteen," he said as she darted past.

Pizza had arrived while she and Mia were in the water. She wrapped herself in a towel, sat down, and reached for a slice. Suddenly, she heard someone bellowing out the birthday song in a badly off-key voice.

"Andy!" She rose up—and then sank down again. "And Johnny."

"Happy birthday to you! Happy birthday to you!" Andy half-warbled, half-garbled. "You smell like a monkey, and you look like one, too!" He burst out laughing as if the botched song was the funniest thing he'd ever heard. Johnny slapped him on the back, guffawing.

"Hilarious," Trey muttered. "I haven't heard that one since first grade."

Helicity set her uneaten pizza on her plate. "Andy, what—"

"No time to talk!" he interrupted. "Time for presents!" He pulled a wrinkled piece of lined paper out of his back pocket and handed it to her with a flourish.

This entitles bearer to a dinner out with her big brother, the paper read. There was an asterisk at the bottom: *Not to be redeemed until her big brother gets his first paycheck!*

"You wanted to spend time with me." Andy jabbed a finger at the paper. "This guarantees you can!"

"Yeah. I got that," Helicity mumbled. The gift should have delighted her. Instead, the hastily scrawled note made her wonder when he'd remembered it was her birthday. An hour ago? Fifteen minutes? Embarrassed, she folded the paper into a tight square and set it carefully on the table. "Thanks. Really."

The others had presents for her, too. Her parents had sent a check—"mad money," her mother called it, to be spent however she wished. Suze and Mia had gone in together on a pair of silver dolphin earrings. Trey's gift was a visit to his mother's lake house the following Tuesday.

"She has a motorboat and a sailboat we can use. It'll be great," he promised.

"Is the invitation just for Helicity?" Mia asked innocently.

"Oh, uh, no, of course not," Trey replied. "You and Sam, too. And Andy, if he's free," he added doubtfully.

"Yeah, maybe," was Andy's only reply.

Sam's present was last. Helicity gasped when she peeled back the wrapping paper. Inside was a framed black-and-white photograph of a lightning bolt.

"It's a still shot from the video I took of the thunderstorm," Sam told her.

"I remember it," Helicity murmured. The image was incredible. It captured the moment the lightning branched across the sky. The clouds were part bright white, part dark shadow, and below them was a tiny sliver of silver ocean.

"Sam, it's stunning," Suze said, clearly impressed. "I wouldn't mind having a copy to display in the Beachside common room. Where guests could see it. *Paying* guests who might like a souvenir that isn't made of plastic or encrusted with seashells," she added significantly.

"No way," Andy said skeptically. "People would buy something like that?"

"Definitely," Suze said.

Helicity only half-heard their exchange. She'd discovered Sam had written something on the back of the photo.

You'll return Lana's lightning bolt someday. But this one is yours to keep.

She traced the words with her fingers, then sought

Sam with her eyes. She wanted to thank him, to tell him how much the picture and inscription meant, but the words couldn't get past the lump in her throat.

She didn't need to say them out loud, though. He drank in her look and with a smile, mouthed back, *You're welcome.*

CHAPTER TWELVE

S am's photograph was the first thing Helicity saw when she woke up the following Tuesday morning. Dangling over the frame was Lana's necklace. She stared at both for a long minute, a small smile playing about her lips.

Mia burst in then, bubbling with excitement for their visit to Trey's lake house. "Which suit goes best with boats?" She held up two equally teeny bikinis.

Helicity laughed. "The boats don't care, and you shouldn't, either."

Mia nodded. "The red one it is, then." She tossed the reject on her bed, then moved into the bathroom to brush her teeth. "Oh, by the way," she said through a mouthful of foam, "did you take some cash from the tip jar? I figured we'd want some money today, but the two tens we got from that nice family last week aren't in there."

"I haven't touched it. Maybe Suze needed it?"

"Yeah, that's probably it." Mia retreated into the bathroom.

Helicity reached for Lana's necklace as she did every morning, then paused. *Better to leave it here than risk losing it,* she thought, Sam's line about returning it to Lana fresh in her mind.

Dressed in swimsuits and cover-ups and with beach bags containing sunscreen, phones, and towels in hand, the girls headed down for breakfast. Suze had the news on with the volume down low.

"So, what's happening in the great wide world?" Mia asked as she took a seat at the kitchen island.

"Not sure about the world," Suze replied, "but there's a bit of trouble around here." She clicked off the television with a frustrated sigh. "Been a rash of break-ins up and down the peninsula. No suspects yet, unfortunately. Police are warning everyone to keep car doors locked and valuables out of sight. Helicity, you should make sure Sam and Andy know about it."

"On it," Helicity said, pulling out her phone and sending both boys a text.

"Besides the robberies," Suze went on, "the only other interesting tidbit is the tropical depression forming out in the Atlantic."

Helicity sat up straighter. "A tropical depression? Where in the Atlantic is it? What are the wind speeds?"

Suze looked amused. "Yeah, sorry, I stopped paying attention after they said they don't know if it will amount to anything. But it is hurricane season, so . . ." She shrugged and smiled. "Nothing you need to worry about at the lake today, anyway."

After breakfast, Helicity and Mia went onto the deck to wait for Sam. Trey was already at his lake house, having gone up with his mother the day before. Andy had made a half promise to join them, but a late-night text crushed Helicity's hope he'd follow through.

Got 2 work, was all he'd written.

"Seriously?" Mia said when she heard. "He couldn't take off one afternoon?"

Helicity rose to her brother's defense. "You know

Andy. He's a responsible guy. He's not going to ditch work just to spend time with his little sister."

"I guess," Mia said grudgingly.

On the deck, Helicity pulled out her phone to look up the tropical depression Suze had mentioned. Six hours earlier, the disorganized cluster of thunderstorms had sustained wind speeds of twenty-seven miles per hour. That number was now at thirty-three, a clear indicator that the storm was gaining energy from the warm waters below. Satellite images showed the thickening clouds swirling counterclockwise, as all such disturbances north of the equator did. Those to the south spun clockwise.

A honk of a car horn snapped her away from the satellite image. Sam had arrived.

"About time," Mia complained as she climbed in the backseat.

"Sorry," he said. "I had to wake Andy up. Then I had to take him to work when Johnny didn't show up."

"Johnny's been driving him?" Helicity asked in surprise, buckling herself in next to Sam.

"Yeah, since last week. Just made sense since they were both going to the same job."

Helicity couldn't argue with that logic, though the idea of Andy spending even more time with Johnny turned her stomach sour. But thoughts like that promised to ruin the day, so she pushed Andy and Johnny from her mind.

Helicity was surprised at how effortlessly Sam navigated his way off the peninsula. Then she remembered he spent most mornings exploring the area before meeting up with her, Mia, and Trey on the beach. They'd set up the campsite together, then play Frisbee or two-on-two soccer on the flats, go beachcombing, or just sit on the sand and talk.

And they swam. After their birthday dunk, Helicity and Mia had rediscovered their love of the water. Sam was a decent swimmer, but Trey moved in the waves as if born to it. Helicity sometimes caught herself admiring his smooth, powerful strokes as his arms sliced through the surf. She also caught Mia raising her eyebrows and smiling at her knowingly when she saw her watching Trey.

"Tell me the truth," Mia said in their room a few nights after the party. "You like Trey."

Helicity traced the seashell pattern on her bed's

comforter. "I do," she confessed. "He's funny. Confident. Easy to be around. And—"

"Easy on the eyes?"

"I was going to say *uncomplicated*." Helicity smiled. "But yeah. Easy on the eyes, too."

But it's more than that, she wrote in her journal later. *I like being with Trey because he's completely unconnected to my past. He's—*

She paused, fumbling for the right word.

He's present. Right here and right now. He listens but doesn't pry into what happened back home. Trey is just . . . here.

She couldn't deny that being with someone who made no demands on her felt good. But she also couldn't deny that her attraction to Sam was as powerful as ever. Had Mia asked about her feelings for him, Helicity would have given a one-word answer: *complicated*.

CHAPTER THIRTEEN

Two hours after leaving the Beachside, Sam pulled into the driveway of a modest two-bedroom cabin on Lake Livingston, the second largest body of freshwater in Texas. Boats of all sorts, from canoes, kayaks, and Jet Skis to sailboats, luxury power craft, and party barges dotted the waves.

Trey bounded out of the house with his mother, a fit middle-aged woman with her son's deep brown eyes and curly blond hair, right behind him. They led their guests to the dock, where two colorful boats bobbed in the water. One was a sailboat with a bright purple hull and a crisp white sail with a number 3 in the center—for *Trey*, Helicity assumed. Next to it was a red-bottomed dinghy with an outboard motor. Both were just big enough for two people.

"It's windy out there today," Mrs. Valdez warned, "so keep your life jackets on."

"We will, Mom." Trey moved to the sailboat.

Sam held out his hand to Helicity and smiled. "Dinghy?"

That smile brought butterflies to life in her stomach. She tried to tamp them down, but when she took his hand, they went crazy.

A fleeting look of disappointment crossed Trey's face. But he shook it off and helped Mia into the sailboat. He guided the craft away from the dock. Wind caught the sail, and he and Mia zipped away toward open water. Helicity admired Trey's masterful maneuvering of the sailboat.

Sam, meanwhile, was struggling to get the dinghy started. "You would think after years of mowing lawns, I'd get this on the first try." He pulled the ripcord attached to the motor so hard he nearly fell off the boat.

"Need help?" Mrs. Valdez yelled from the back porch, where she had retreated, glass of wine in hand.

"No, no . . . I . . . have . . . got this," Sam replied through gritted teeth. The engine finally purred to life.

Helicity sat sideways in the dinghy's bow, her legs tucked underneath her and her orange life vest snug around her neck and upper body. She tried not to think about the last time she'd worn one. But she couldn't stop the images. Sam, dazed and bleeding from his forehead, clinging to the top of Lana's SUV. Sam being pulled on a line through the water to shore. Lana rushing out to get her, gripping her life vest, trying to tell her something, vanishing beneath the churning waves. The nightmarish memories flooded her brain with the same powerful force as the floodwater itself.

"Hey. You still with me?"

Sam's voice brought her back. She reached for her necklace, then remembered she'd left it in her room. She closed her eyes briefly, visualizing its lightning bolt. This time, the necklace mingled in her mind with Sam's photograph.

"Yeah." She opened her eyes and smiled. "I'm totally with you."

Sam raised his eyebrows, then guided the dinghy farther from shore.

Out in the open water, the wind plucked at Helicity's hair. Grinning, Sam reached forward, captured a strand between his fingers, and gave it a quick tug.

The water was choppier the farther out they got. The sun played peekaboo with the clouds, making the waves sparkle and darken by turns. They putted around for a while, neither saying much, both content to simply be.

Then Helicity broke the quiet. "Sam, where did you go after you left the hospital?"

Sam cut the motor. Waves rocked the boat, making a hollow thump as they slapped against the hull. It was a desolate sound that matched the faraway look on Sam's face.

"You remember that old guy at the nursing home where my dad works?" he finally said. "The one who bought your Memorial Day tornado photos?"

She nodded. She also remembered that Sam had sold him those photos without her permission. But she didn't mention that now.

"He's a weird old dude, Mr. Chalmers, but . . . well, I like the guy. He loved being out in nature, seeing stormy weather, like me. Like us. Anyway, when I got home after the hospital, Dad told me Mr. Chalmers wasn't doing too well. I knew his kids lived too far away to visit. So, I went instead. Every day for a week, actually."

"Did he . . . is he . . . ?"

"He improved a little bit each day, thank God," he said. "That's why I kept going. Seeing him get better gave me hope that Lana would, too, someday." He gave a little laugh then. "He was feeling so much better, in fact, that he told me to stop coming around."

"Really?"

"Yeah, I told you he was weird. But he's special, too. My new digital camera? He gave it to me. Just *gave* it to me." He shook his head in wonderment. "He said he wasn't sure when he'd get outdoors again. So, he asked me to bring the outdoors to him."

"Camping," Helicity guessed. "You went camping and shot videos and photos to share with him."

"He tucked a wad of cash inside the camera case. He refused to let me give it back. So I made good use of it. Bought the camping stuff secondhand, then headed up to the Upper Peninsula and worked my way down the shore of Lake Michigan. The camera is loaded with features—slo-mo, remote start from my phone, low light, you name it—so getting great footage was a cinch." He paused. "But I'm pretty sure Mr. Chalmers had an ulterior motive for sending me off that didn't include videography."

He let his hand fall into the waves. V's streamed from his fingertips. "He wanted me to have the freedom to process what had happened. And I did. Being alone in the wilderness like that . . . it gave me time to think. Get some clarity, as they say." He glanced at her. "The thing I kept coming back to the most? How wrong I was to leave without seeing you. So, when I neared home, I went to your house, only to discover you'd come here."

She bit her lip. "You didn't have to come all this way to see me. You could have just texted or called."

He tilted his head to one side. "No. I had to see you in person. To see for myself that you were okay."

"I am okay, Sam," she said quietly. "Or at least, I'm getting there."

"Me too. I never thought I would, but . . . yeah." He shook his head. "That's the first time I've said that out loud. But I feel like I can tell you anything . . . Fifteen." He gave her a mischievous smile.

Just then, a speedboat pulling a water skier raced

by. The skier slalomed expertly back and forth across the boat's wake, then suddenly swerved toward them. An arc of water blasted up from the ski. Helicity caught the drenching spray in her face full force. She sputtered and gasped in shock as the speedboat raced off, the driver and a female passenger hooting with laughter, the skier pumping his fist.

"Idiots!" Sam bellowed after them. He crouch-walked over to Helicity. "Are you okay?"

"Yeah." She dashed the water off her face. "I must look like a drowned rat."

"You ask me, you never looked better."

Sam's voice sounded odd. She looked up—and found herself staring into his eyes. For two beats of her heart, the world stopped moving. Sam's face was so near to hers, she could feel the magnetism electrify-ing the air between them. Her lips parted. He leaned in closer, eyes still on hers.

Suddenly, something on the horizon stole Helicity's attention. She blinked, not sure what she was seeing at first. When she figured it out, her stomach lurched.

"Sam," she said urgently, "we need to find Mia and Trey and get to shore. *Now*."

CHAPTER FOURTEEN

An ominous dark cloud sat like a hulking beast over the distant shore. But as frightening as it looked, the cloud wasn't what had Helicity urging Sam to power up the motor and find their friends. It was the wind.

When they'd first started out onto the lake, the wind had been a steady breeze. But while Sam was telling her about Mr. Chalmers, it had changed. Now it blew in erratic gusts that were more frequent and gaining in strength with every passing moment. If what she suspected was true . . .

"It's not a thunderstorm, Sam!"

Sam looked at Helicity quizzically. "Then what is it?"

"I—I think it's a derecho!"

Sam's eyes widened with fear. "Oh, God. If you're right—if Mia and Trey get caught in it in that little sailboat—" He clipped off the rest of the sentence and fired up the motor—this time on the first try.

A derecho was not just *a* thunderstorm, but a long line of them, an army of thunderstorms. When that army organized, the front line bowed out and became a highly destructive windstorm. Like tornadoes, derechos produced wind gusts that could exceed 120 miles per hour. They could do more damage and over a larger area than weak tornadoes could, because instead of spinning, their winds marched straight forward, blasting over everything in their path—including boats.

At the far side of the lake, sailboats were rocking and tipping, threatening to capsize. Closer by, motorboats were racing toward the docks, causing near collisions as their drivers jockeyed to escape the mounting waves. Jet-Skiers wove in and out among the boats in their quest to get to land.

Suddenly, a fierce gust pummeled the surface of the water near their dinghy. A wave crashed into the boat's side, and water sloshed over the edge, drowning Helicity's beach bag as the tiny craft fought to stay upright. Sam steered as best he could while Helicity searched the sailboats for Trey and Mia.

"There!" She spotted the distinctive bright purple hull and number 3. The boat was heeling over and back at dangerous angles. Trey was moving about, trying to drop sail to keep them from capsizing. But his skill on the sail was no match for these winds.

"Faster, Sam!"

The dinghy bounced over the waves, the bow rising up and slapping down with dull, jarring thuds.

"Helicity!"

Mia's panicked voice made Helicity's stomach clutch. "Hold on! We're coming!" She turned to Sam. "Is our motor strong enough to pull the sailboat behind us?"

Sam's lips tightened. "I don't think so!"

"Then you'll have to get close enough for them to jump into our boat!"

Helicity wasn't sure the dinghy would hold them all, and she could tell Sam wasn't, either. But she was out of ideas—and from the way the waves were humping and rolling higher and harder, she was also running out of time.

As they drew near to the sailboat, another bigger motorboat cut through the waves ahead of them. With a shock, Helicity realized it was the speedboat. Its three occupants weren't laughing now.

"You need help?" the driver shouted.

"Can you tow that sailboat?"

The girl shot her friends a doubtful look, but the skier crab-walked to the swim deck in the stern with a length of rope. Trey was still trying to lower the sail, so Mia crouched in readiness to catch the line. But just as the boy threw, a blast of wind whipped the boom from Trey's grasp. The beam caught Mia across the shoulders with a sickening thump. She toppled forward and disappeared in the lake.

"*Mia!*"

Helicity scrambled up.

"No!" Sam lunged forward and grabbed her life vest. "Don't, Helicity!"

"Let me go! She'll drown!"

"And you might, too, if you go in after her!"

Mia bobbed to the surface, gulping for air and sobbing. Her life jacket held her head above the water, but it couldn't stop the waves from crashing into her face.

"Help . . . me . . . please!" she gasped. Her fingers clutched at empty air.

"The line!" Helicity shrieked at the speedboat. "For God's sake, throw her the rope!"

The boy reeled in the rope hand over hand and threw it toward Mia. It fell far from her reach. And her struggles were getting weaker.

Helicity whirled on Sam. "I have to help her!"

He stared at her for a long moment. Then he let go of her life jacket.

She leaped feetfirst into the water, arms outstretched to keep her from plunging under. With powerful kicks, she battled the waves to reach Mia's side. She grabbed her with one arm and thrust the other above the waves. "Throw me the line!" she cried, thrashing her legs to stay in one place. "Now!"

This time, the rope reached its target. Helicity swiveled her wrist to wrap the end around it, then held on tight. "Pull!"

The waves fought against them, but at last the

passengers dragged them onto the swim deck. Mia rolled into a fetal position, coughing up water and choking on her sobs. Helicity lay next to her. Her chest was heaving, and her lungs burned. The skin on her wrist was rubbed raw. But they were safe. Alive.

For now.

"Get us out of here!" the girl yelled. The driver gunned the motor and headed for the nearest stretch of shore.

"Wait!" Helicity shouted. "My friends!"

But the motor drowned out her cries. Heart in her throat, she watched Sam swing the dinghy as near to the sailboat as he could. Trey jumped on board. The dinghy rocked dangerously. Then they took off after the speedboat.

And not a moment too soon. Behind them, a gust of wind tore at the boat's sail. Then a wave flipped the tiny craft on its side—a stark reminder that they weren't out of danger yet.

When they finally reached shore, Helicity helped Mia out of the boat. Together, they slogged through the shallows and collapsed in the sand. They lay there for a minute, the winds raging around them. Then Helicity forced herself to sit up.

"Sam? Trey?"

"Over here," Trey responded. He, Sam, and the teens from the speedboat were huddled beneath a tree. "We're okay . . . mostly."

"Good." Helicity struggled up. "Because we need to get out of here. Fast."

"What? Why?" asked the girl.

A powerful gust of wind bent a nearby tree. The trunk snapped in half with an ear-shattering *crack*. "That's why!"

Sam was already on his feet. "This way!" he yelled, waving them toward a footpath that led through a sparsely wooded area. "Come on!"

Another wind gust blew a dead branch out of a tree above him. He dodged as the limb shattered in an explosion of sharp sticks and twigs where he'd been standing.

"Are you crazy?" the girl cried. "If we go in there, we'll get our heads bashed in! Or worse!"

Helicity knew she couldn't do anything about the "or worse." But she had an idea to protect their heads.

"Our life vests." She whipped hers from around her neck and put it on her head like an oversize hat.

"I've got something better!" The driver started tossing out seat cushions and beach towels. Within seconds, everyone was swaddled in makeshift protective gear.

Sam pushed aside an overgrown bush blocking the footpath and led the way, with Trey and Helicity helping Mia, and the others following close behind. A sudden rain turned the ground into a soggy, sucking quicksand. The girl stepped on something that made her cry out in pain.

She swore when she saw what it was. "Broken glass!" She swore some more as the speedboat driver tried to extract the shard.

"Hold still, Summer!" he railed at her. "There!" He threw the glass into the underbrush. Summer hobbled on, leaving a trail of blood behind her.

The path took them to a small wooden cabin. It was obviously abandoned, most of its windows boarded up and covered with graffiti. The front door sagged on its hinges. But it was better than nothing. Helicity pushed in front of the others and yanked open the door. The whole crew filed inside behind her.

Except for a few simple plank shelves falling off the walls, the interior had been stripped clean of furnishings. But something was clearly living there. The smell of decay and animal droppings was overpowering, like a neglected zoo enclosure whose occupants had been left to rot.

"Oh, *God*." Gagging, Summer covered her mouth and nose with her towel. "How long are we going to have to stay here?"

Sam looked at Helicity. "If this is a derecho, it could be at least half an hour."

"Please tell me one of you has a cell phone!" Summer said.

"Sorry," Helicity said shortly. "I was a little busy." *Just saving my best friends' lives and probably yours*, she added silently as she piled the seat cushions together. Sam had left his phone in his car, and Trey's and Mia's were lost with the sailboat. "But hey, look on the bright side."

"*What* bright side?" Summer whined.

Helicity eased Mia down onto the pillow pile. "You're alive."

CHAPTER FIFTEEN

The words were barely out of Helicity's mouth when *boom!* Something outside pounded against the cabin like a giant fist. The skier screamed and hurled himself into the arms of his friends. They looked so ridiculous clutching one another that Helicity nearly laughed out loud.

Mia's trembling voice stopped her. "What was that?"

"It's debris from the storm," Helicity told her. "Don't worry. We'll be safe in here." *I hope.*

Crash! Boom! Thwack!

Wreckage battered the already crumbling cabin, shaking it to the foundation and sending Helicity's mind back to the tornado. She muttered her mantra in her mind to fight against the rising panic. *I'm a survivor, not a victim. I'm a survivor, not a victim.* This time it was not cheesy, Helicity knew that. This time it was more than valid.

A cloud of thick, choking dust filled the air, then her nostrils, making her cough. An old bird's nest with broken eggshells fell from the ceiling rafters and rolled at their feet. Howling wind tore at the boarded-up windows and rattled the door. The cabin felt like it was going to implode. So did her fear.

Then Sam pressed his hand into hers and squeezed. "Deep breaths. In through the nose. Out through the mouth," he murmured in her ear.

She caught his eye. And remembered the time in Lana's office after the tornado when he'd witnessed her spiraling out of control. Lana had sent him out of the room before helping her regain control. But had Sam heard Lana's whispered instructions after all? If so, she was glad. Listening to him now calmed her inner turbulence. She coughed again, then focused on breathing slowly and steadily. Her mind cleared, and her strength returned.

Then suddenly, it went eerily quiet. Summer and the friends stared at one other, hope blooming on their faces.

"It's over!" The speedboat driver jumped to his feet and ran to look out the last remaining window.

"No!" Helicity yelled. "Stay down!"

Her cry saved him. As he turned to look at her, a gust more powerful than any they had heard before blasted the window. It exploded into thousands of razor-sharp fragments. Had he not looked away, that deadly shower would have hit him directly in his eyes.

Instead, the flying shards embedded in his cheek, ear, and hair. He shrieked and fell to his knees, cupping a hand to his face. Blood oozed from multiple pinprick cuts and dripped from one particularly deep slash on his jawline. He rocked back and forth, moaning.

Summer and the skier stared at him in horror. But when the boy made a move to help his friend, Summer grabbed his arm. "No! Don't leave me!"

Sam growled in disgust and pushed himself to his feet.

"Wait!" Helicity cried. She thrust a beach towel

into his hand. "Take this!" Helicity and Sam's new deal, not being selfish or stupid, was implied.

He scuttled toward the wounded boy. Halfway there, a loud *crack* split the air. Then a thunderous crash as a giant tree smashed through the roof.

"Sam!" Helicity screamed.

What happened next seemed to play out in slow motion. The rafters caught the massive trunk—only for a heartbeat, but long enough for Trey to launch himself at Sam and shove him out of harm's way. Then the rafters gave way and the tree crashed on top of him.

For one horrible moment, Helicity was sure Trey was dead. Then he let out a shriek of pain that pierced through the wind's howls.

Helicity raced to Trey's side. Sam threw the towel to the speedboat driver and skidded up beside her. "Oh. God," he breathed as he stared at Trey in horror. Helicity's hands flew to her mouth to keep herself from screaming.

The tree was top-heavy with thick, stout branches. Those branches had stopped the trunk just short of crushing him. Trey might have even escaped unscathed . . . if not for one short, jagged limb. Like a wooden spear, it had stabbed into the back of his thigh, pinning him where he'd fallen. Blood dripped from the wound, running in bright red rivulets down his bare leg to form a small puddle.

A puddle that was spreading wider by the second.

Trey groaned and made a move as if to crawl forward.

"No! Don't!" Sam cried.

Trey's eyes bugged with pain, then rolled up into his head. He passed out face-first in a pile of splinters and broken glass.

"His leg. The blood," Helicity choked.

"We have to get the tree off him," Sam said urgently.

They tried shifting the trunk themselves, but it was just too enormous. Helicity glanced at the speedboat driver. No. He had his own problems to deal with. Mia was in no shape to help, either. That left Summer and the skier.

"You two, get over here! Now!" she demanded.

"And have a tree land on me? No way!" Summer yelled.

The skier stared at her, then shook his head. "You're a waste."

He started toward them, then backtracked and ripped two shelves from the wall. He stacked the boards under the trunk in front of Trey, then positioned himself under the top edge of one of the sides.

Sam got under the other side of the boards. "Helicity, take hold of Trey. When I say so, pull him free."

Helicity crouched low and gently looped her arms under Trey's shoulders. This was the closest she had ever been to him. How horribly ironic, Helicity thought. The one time she has someone that isn't related to her tumultuous past, they are becoming part of her stormy present and future. There was no time for admiration or self-loathing. Fear and adrenaline set her heart pounding in her chest.

To the boy, Sam said, "On three. One. Two. Three."

Heavy rain pelted them through the gaping roof as they leveraged their shoulders under the boards, pushing up and straining to lift the tree. The old wooden planks bent and groaned in protest. Helicity held her breath and closed her eyes. When she peered through, she saw physics at work.

The trunk moved. The jagged branch, coated with

Trey's blood, skin, and bits of flesh, pulled out of his leg inch by horrifying inch.

"Get ready, Fifteen!"

The boys gave one big push. The tip of the branch came free.

"Now!"

Helicity pulled. Her foot slipped in something wet. *Please let that be rainwater,* she begged, *not Trey's blood!*

"Go!" Sam groaned. *"Go-go-go!"*

She backpedaled frantically and dragged Trey free just as the skier's side of the boards snapped in two. Sam's fell from his shoulder. The tree thudded to the floor, shaking the cabin on impact. Helicity was shaking, too. Then someone thrust a towel into her hand.

"To stop his bleeding," Mia sobbed from behind her.

Helicity pressed the fabric into the puncture wound and held it there. Sam tore another towel into strips. Helicity swapped her blood-soaked towel for a fresh one, then used Sam's strips to secure it in place.

"Should we tie on a tourniquet or something?" the skier asked.

Helicity shook her head. "Do you know how? I

don't want it to hurt more than help." She moved next to Mia. "Mia, I need these cushions to elevate his leg."

Mia rolled off instantly. Helicity stacked the cushions and very gently eased Trey's leg onto the pile. "That's all we can do for him for now," she murmured, sitting back on her heels. "That, and hope that someone finds us soon."

Mia crept forward to dab a wet piece of towel over Trey's forehead. He stirred, moaning, then stilled.

Outside, the rain hammered at the cabin walls. The wind shrieked and whistled across the hole in the roof. Then, after what seemed like an eternity, the rain lightened. The wind's fury lessened. Finally, a hush fell over everything like a blanket.

Something beat against the cabin door, startling them. Three times, then again.

"Hey! Anybody in there?" a deep voice yelled.

Summer sprang to her feet. "Help! Yes! Please, help me!" With no energy to add "help us," the rest of the group simply ignored Summer's narcissistic shouts.

The door cracked open and an old man peered in. He took one look at Trey and the speedboat driver, then pulled out his cell phone and dialed 9-1-1.

"It's over," Mia whispered. She clutched Helicity's hand. "It's over."

Helicity bowed her head and squeezed back. "And we survived."

CHAPTER SIXTEEN

"Helicity. Helicity, wake up."

Helicity groaned and opened her eyes a crack. Harsh overhead lights made her vision swim. She squinted to bring the person in front of her into focus. "Suze?" she croaked. "Suze. Where am I?"

"The hospital," Suze replied. Her elfin features were pinched with worry, but she managed a smile. "Well, the couch in the waiting room of the Bolivar hospital, to be exact. How are you feeling?"

Helicity licked her parched lips. "My head is pounding. My throat is killing me. And the smell from this couch is making me feel sick." She struggled to sit up.

"Easy does it," Suze advised, quickly sweeping her arm around Helicity's shoulders to steady her. "There. Better?"

For a split second, Helicity was better. Then it all came rocketing back to her. Not just the derecho, but the wailing sirens, flashing lights, and urgent voices of the first responders. Questions. Answers. More questions. A blanket around her shoulders. Her sodden beach bag rescued from the dinghy and thrust in her hand. And blood on her feet and legs. Trey's blood.

She seized Suze's arm. "Oh, God. Trey!"

Suze covered Helicity's hand with her own. "He's okay, Helicity. They transported him to a hospital near Lake Livingston. He lost a lot of blood and will need a ton of stitches. But his mother says he's going to be fine. Mia will be, too. She's here, getting checked out."

"And Sam?"

"Right behind you." Sam came around a corner with a bottle of water. Exhaustion had punched deep circles under his eyes. Like her, he was still wearing his dirt- and blood-streaked clothes. "Here. I thought you might need this."

"Thanks." Helicity drank thirstily, then wiped her lips and looked up at him quizzically. "The last thing I remember is getting in the back of your car with Mia after the police officer dropped us at the Valdezes' cabin."

Sam gave a little laugh. "Yeah, you both fell asleep while I was calling Suze. You stayed asleep when I carried you in here. Mia got the star treatment with a wheelchair ride."

Helicity flushed to her roots imagining Sam holding her in his arms and silently gave thanks that she'd put on her cover-up before getting into his car.

Suze told her she'd called her parents. Helicity was about to ask if Andy knew what had happened when she saw her brother walking down the hallway. Shoulders hunched and hands shoved deep in his pockets, he seemed unaware of them.

"Andy!" she cried. "Andy, over here!"

His head snapped up. "Helicity?" Confusion contorted his features. He glanced around and hurried over, then stopped short, his eyes widening. "What the hell happened to you?"

Now it was Helicity's turn to be confused. She knew she and Sam looked like they had been through war.

And they had, in a sense. But wouldn't Andy know why they looked so wretched?

"The storm," she said in bewilderment. "The derecho. I—we—were caught in it." In the cabin, she'd been too laser-focused on the immediate trauma to think about the bigger picture. But now the reality of what had happened—and what might have happened—sank in. Her throat suddenly tightened. Tears sprang to her eyes. She reached out her arms. *"Andy."*

In an instant, he was folding her into a fierce hug. She sobbed quietly for a long moment, then drew in a long, deep breath. Her nose instinctively searched for Andy's familiar, comforting scent. But instead, a sour stench like mildewed towels layered with rank body odor assaulted her nostrils. And something sharper, too—a whiff of vomit, strong enough to curdle her stomach.

She pulled back and stared at him. Andy's eyes were red-rimmed, she saw now, his cheeks and chin stubbled with beard, and his wavy hair hanging in lank, greasy strings.

He noticed her expression and moved away. "Sorry. Haven't had a chance to shower today," he said gruffly.

"Now, will you please tell me what's going on?"

Helicity opened her mouth, but no words came out. Sam laid a gentle hand on her arm. "I got this." He outlined everything that had happened. "I tried to call you. Text you," he finished. "But I guess you didn't see the messages."

When Andy shook his head, Helicity found her voice. "I don't understand. If you didn't know we were here, then why did you come?"

In reply, Andy unzipped his hoodie and exposed his right arm. A thick bandage, stark white next to his yellowed, pit-stained tank top, covered most of his shoulder. "I fell off a ladder at work. Got a nasty gash and a few bumps and bruises. I wouldn't have come in except . . . well, it's my bad arm. But I'm fine."

He started to laugh, then winced. "Okay, maybe not *fine*," he admitted, gingerly pulling up the hoodie's sleeve. "But better than Mia or Trey, it sounds like."

"Trey's in good hands, and the doctor says Mia's lucky," Suze told them. "A few inches higher, and she would have taken the boom in the back of her neck. Or her head."

Andy gave a low whistle. "That would have been

a concussion for sure." He tapped his temple. "Been there. Had that. Not fun."

Helicity nodded, remembering when Andy had taken a hard helmet hit to the head during a football game two years earlier. *Had his bell rung*, was how his father had put it. Her brother had been forced to sit out a few weeks until his doctor deemed him fit to return. He'd been a beast to live with. But once he got back on the field, he returned to his usual sunny self.

"Mia's going to be hurting pretty hard for a few days," Andy said now. "Hopefully just bruises and stuff, though. Poor kid."

"Andrew Dunlap?" a woman called from behind a Plexiglas-enclosed countertop. "Your prescription is ready."

Helicity blinked. "Whoa, what? I thought you said you were fine."

Andy stood up. "Just some pain meds. I said I didn't need them, but . . . doctor's orders." He shrugged, then flinched again and touched his injured arm. "Maybe she was right after all." As he moved to the counter, he added, "You know, Mia might need some of these, too. Sounds like she's worse off than I am."

When Andy returned with his prescription, Suze got to her feet. "I need to get back to Mia. She's getting X-rays," she informed Helicity. "We're going to be a while yet, so you three should go on back to the Beachside. Get yourselves cleaned up. And buy yourselves something to eat on the way."

She unzipped her purse and withdrew her wallet. Inside was a thick layer of bills. She pulled out two twenties and gave them to Helicity. When Helicity tried to refuse, Suze captured her face with her hand and fixed her with a searching look. "Helicity. What you did for Mia . . . I owe you more than this. Much, much more."

Tears welled up in Helicity's eyes. "You've given me so much already, Suze. You don't owe me anything. Ever."

Suze smiled, then turned to the boys. "You two stay the night, okay? My guests canceled at the last minute. And I think Helicity would like it if you were there."

Sam nodded gratefully and Andy grunted. Suze left then to return to Mia.

"You guys ready to go?" Sam asked.

"Hang on," Andy replied, pulling out a phone. "I gotta let Johnny know I don't need a ride."

Helicity frowned when she saw his phone. "That's not your cell. Where'd you get that?"

"What, this? Oh. It's for work." Understanding dawned on his face. "That's why I didn't get Sam's messages. I left my other phone in my duffel." He shook his head at his own stupidity, then wandered off to make his call.

Helicity looked at Sam. "Why would he need a phone for a temporary painting job?"

Sam shrugged. "Who knows."

Despite Suze's insistence that they return to the Beachside, Helicity was reluctant to leave without seeing Mia. But exhaustion won out. She fought to keep her eyes open on the ride. Her feet felt leaden as she climbed the stairs to the deck and then to the loft. There, she sank down onto her bed as the full weight of the day's events pressed down on her. She wanted nothing more than to lie down and sleep. One look in the mirror told her a shower had to come first.

She caught sight of the swimsuit Mia had tossed aside that morning. For some reason, the colorful scraps of material jogged something in her memory. Something Mia had whispered to her just before she'd nodded off on the way to the hospital.

I can't believe you jumped in to save me.

Helicity carried those words with her into the bathroom, turning them over and over as dirt, leaves, and dried blood washed down the shower drain. She'd been haunted by the same thought herself after the tornado. After the flood. After first Andy, then Lana, risked their lives for her.

Why? she'd wondered. *Why did they put themselves in such danger?*

In some warped part of her brain, she'd wished they hadn't. Because then Andy would be packing for college, and Lana might still be out chasing storms with Ray.

But now she understood. They came after her because they cared about her. Loved her. And if someone you love is in trouble, you don't choose to save them. You just do it.

Helicity didn't think she had any tears left after crying in Andy's arms in the hospital. But as she toweled off and dressed, fresh ones trickled down her cheeks. They weren't tears of fear and anxiety, though. They were tears of shared love. Tears of grateful joy.

Good tears.

CHAPTER SEVENTEEN

A soft knock startled Helicity back to the present. "Fifteen? Can I come in?"

"Hang on." She dashed the wet from her cheeks and opened the door. Sam's hair was damp, and he was dressed in a clean T-shirt and shorts. Bright red nicks and raw scrapes marred the skin on his arms, legs, and feet. A new bruise on his shoulder, courtesy of the plank, peeked out from one sleeve.

She sat on the bed and he took the floor.

"You okay?" He held up a hand before she could answer. "Sorry. Stupid question. Of course you're not."

"No, but I'm not losing it, either, Sam. Not anymore,

anyway." She drew her knees up to her chest. "What about you? How are you feeling?"

He blew out a long breath. "Incredibly lucky, that's how I'm feeling. If Trey hadn't shoved me out of the way . . ." He shook his head in disbelief. "He saved my life. I'll never be able to repay him." He looked at her. "By my count, that makes two people I owe my life to."

Helicity knew he meant her, when she had freed him from the wreck of Lana's SUV. She moved to the floor next to him. "You don't owe me anything. Or Trey, either. He did what he did because . . . well, because that's the kind of guy he is."

"And you? Why did you rescue me, Fifteen?" His voice was hoarse and barely louder than a breath. He nudged his bruised shoulder against hers. And kept it there.

She stilled, acutely aware of his body next to hers. Of his long-fingered hands dangling over his bent knees. Of his chest rising and falling with breath. Of the warmth of his skin where it touched hers. Of the fact that they were alone in her room.

A jaunty ring tone jerked her out of the sudden

sensations threatening to overwhelm her. She lurched to her knees and grabbed her phone from her bedside table. Her fingers tangled up in the chain of Lana's necklace, and the phone fell from her grasp. It landed faceup, the selfie of her by the dolphin statue with Trey on the screen, announcing that Trey was calling.

Sam blinked when he saw the photo. But he didn't say anything, just passed her the phone.

"Trey?" Helicity put the call on speakerphone so Sam could hear. "Is that you?"

"Heliztee!" Trey's voice was overly loud and slightly slurred. "Yeeahhh, itz me! I got snitches. No. Wait." He guffawed with laughter. "Not *snitches*. Stitches! Like a li'l ol' train track on my leg. Woo-woo!" He made a sound like a train whistle.

Helicity and Sam exchanged bemused glances. "Um, Trey, are you okay?" Helicity asked.

"Oh, I'm fine. More than fine, I'm— Ah! Give that back! I'm talking to my girl!"

There was a muffled sound, and then Mrs. Valdez came on the line. "Helicity? I'm sorry about that. Trey seems to be having a rather strong reaction to the pain medication they gave him."

"Woo-woo!" Trey cried in the background.

"Shush, you," Mrs. Valdez chastised her son. "He called you when I stepped out of the room. Again, Helicity, my apologies."

"It's okay, Mrs. Valdez, really. How's he doing?"

"Well, aside from twenty stitches in the back of his leg, the doctors say he is very, very fortunate. A few inches one way or the other and that tree branch might have hit something major. They passed along praise for you and Sam, by the way." Her voice turned tremulous with emotion. "Said your quick action probably saved his life. For which his father and I will be forever in your debt."

Sam stared at the floor and shook his head. Helicity understood what he was saying without words: Trey wouldn't have needed saving if he hadn't risked his own life for Sam.

Mrs. Valdez cleared her throat. "Anyway. He'll stay overnight just to be sure there's no infection, then be back home tomorrow sometime."

"Could we come by and visit?"

"Of course. I'll have him call you. Assuming he's more himself by then, that is."

As Helicity hung up, she could still hear Trey in the background protesting. The faint sound of "my girl" echoing in her head, she turned to Sam, who pretended not to have heard that part. Or at least that's what she felt his look away was all about. Then she heard voices downstairs. "Mia's back!" She got to her feet. Sam remained on the floor, his brow creased as if he was deep in thought. "Sam? You coming?"

"What? Oh, yeah."

Darkness had fallen while she and Sam were upstairs. Now stars sprinkled the night sky outside the picture windows, and the waxing moon was just showing over the horizon.

Helicity rushed over to her friend with her arms wide but stopped short in front of her. "I want to hug you, but I don't want to hurt you."

Mia gave her a wan smile. "You sound like a bad country-western song. Here's another lyric. 'I might be bruised, but I'm not broken. So hug me, baby, hug me.'"

Helicity wrapped her arms around her and held on tight. When she finally let go, Suze helped Mia upstairs, returning a short while later to announce that her niece was down for the count.

"I just hope she sleeps right through the night," Suze said, falling into an easy chair with a deep sigh.

Andy, showered and smelling much better, wandered in from the kitchen. "Did they give you something for the pain if she needs it? The first night after my car accident was the worst for me. I wouldn't have gotten through it without my meds."

Suze held up an orange prescription bottle and shook it. "I've got these, just in case. But Mia wanted to stick with an over-the-counter pill." She put the bottle on the side table and glanced at Helicity. "She said you had bizarre nightmares when you took the heavy-duty stuff, and she didn't want that to happen to her."

"She's right, I did." Helicity shivered, recalling the bad dreams her drug-fogged mind had produced after the flash flood. "I think Mom tossed the rest of them after I told her."

"Probably," Andy agreed.

"You never had problems with your painkillers, though, right?" Helicity asked her brother.

"Me? Nah. But then I'm like, what, five times bigger and stronger than you. So, they wouldn't affect me as much."

Suze looked at him curiously. "I'm not sure pre-scription painkillers work like that." She stood up. "I'm heading to bed. Helicity, come get me if you or Mia need anything in the night." She disappeared into her bedroom.

Andy stretched luxuriously. "Ah! Sleeping in air-conditioning. Heaven."

Sam shook his head. "I keep telling you to unzip the window flaps, let some fresh air into your tent."

"And I keep telling you that I like my privacy." Andy jerked up out of his chair, filled a glass of water in the kitchen, and retreated to his room with a cursory "G'night." When the door closed, Sam turned to Helicity.

"Is everything okay with him?"

Helicity blinked in surprise. "Andy? Yeah, I think so. Why?"

Sam tossed a throw pillow from hand to hand. "It's just . . . well, he's been acting kind of weird since we got here."

"Weird how?"

"He gets up and leaves in the middle of the night, and then sleeps like the dead in the morning. I hate waking him up because he always bites my head off—and then he bites my head off again for not waking him up sooner."

Helicity stared at him. "Where does he go at night?" She groaned. "Not hanging with Johnny, I hope."

Sam made a face that told her that's exactly who he thought Andy was with. "Maybe I'm way off base, Fifteen, but I can't help wondering if Andy is having some . . . I don't know. Problems. Like, emotional problems. Because of the tornado, I mean, and the big question mark about his future."

"Emotional problems? Andy?" Helicity scoffed. "No way. He's too strong."

"But has he changed since the tornado?" Sam persisted.

She fidgeted in her chair, feeling edgy and defensive all of a sudden. "He's been a little grumpy, I guess. He could stand to shower more often." She spread her hands. "As for his sleep stuff, you heard him about the air-conditioning. He probably can't sleep in the heat. No big deal."

"And Johnny?"

She sighed and dropped her hands back in her lap.

"I don't like him any more than you do. But Andy can take care of himself. And besides, I'd know if he was having trouble with anything."

"How?"

"Because he tells me everything, that's how," she said shortly. She got to her feet. "Listen, it's been a long day. I'm going to bed."

"Fifteen."

She paused with her foot on the bottom stair. "What?"

"I know how much you love your brother. How much you look up to him. But . . . Andy might not be as strong as you think." He moved to her side and searched her face. "And nobody tells anyone everything. Nobody." He continued to his room without another word.

Upstairs in her bed, Helicity laced her fingers behind her head and frowned at the ceiling.

Sam is way off base, she thought furiously. *Andy is fine.*

Images of her brother in the hospital that afternoon flashed across her mind. His red eyes, unshaven face, and stringy hair. The smell clinging to his clothes.

How he'd walked, head down and hands shoved into his pockets.

Andy might not be as strong as you think. And nobody tells anyone everything.

Sam's words wormed into her brain. She tried to block them out, but they kept returning. Could Andy be in trouble? And if so, why was he hiding it from her?

Finally, beyond frustrated and with the glowing red numbers on the digital clock showing it was well past midnight, she decided to head downstairs for a cup of chamomile tea to soothe her jangling nerves. She crept out of bed and tiptoed out to the landing.

And froze when she heard the tinkle of breaking glass.

CHAPTER EIGHTEEN

Someone's breaking into the house.

Helicity ducked behind the half wall and squeezed her eyes shut. Blood from her racing heart pulsed in her ears. She forced herself to take a deep, silent breath. Held it and listened for movement.

All was quiet.

She let the air out of her lungs slowly and noiselessly, then inched her way up to a crouch and peered over the wall.

An intruder stood in the open doorway to the deck. The dim light from the crescent moon cast him in silhouette. That same light glinted on the broken glass scattered on the floor at his feet. Otherwise, the deck was shrouded in darkness. Her stomach clutched when she realized he must have done something to the motion detectors. She tried to see his face, but it was shadowed by his dark hoodie and the night.

He tilted his head, listening. Then he stole into the common room and wove soundlessly between two easy chairs. He paused for a moment, then snatched something from the side table and jammed it into his pocket. Then he slunk farther into the house.

Helicity ducked down again and made herself small in the corner wall by the stairs.

Please don't come up, she begged silently. *Please don't come up.*

She heard the soft but unmistakable *zztttt* of a zipper being unzipped. She swallowed hard. *Suze's purse.* She listened closer and caught the light *clink* of glass on the countertop. The tip jar, she realized. It sat by the sink in plain sight. Easy pickings, though the money within couldn't have topped fifty dollars.

Footfalls lighter than a cat's paws told her he was on the move again. Out of the kitchen. Past the bottom of the loft stairs. Through the common room. And out the back door.

Helicity sat unmoving, barely daring to breathe, until she was absolutely certain he was gone. Then she raced to her bedroom and grabbed her phone. The digital clock told her less than five minutes had passed since she got out of bed.

It felt like a lifetime.

"Helicity?" Mia said sleepily. "What's going on?"

"Trouble," Helicity answered. She ran downstairs to Suze's room and pounded on her door, fingers shaking as she dialed 9-1-1. The door opened at the same time the call was answered, so she only had to say it once: "We've been robbed."

For the second time in less than twelve hours, Helicity was surrounded by flashing blue lights. The police had arrived within minutes of her call. Suze, Mia, and Sam stood by her as she told an officer what she had witnessed.

Andy appeared midway through—not from his bedroom, though he was in his usual sleep attire of a T-shirt and shorts, but from the back stairs to the deck. He started toward Helicity only to find his way blocked by the policeman's stiff arm. "Hey! What the hell!" he cried in protest.

"Let him by, please," Suze intervened. "He's family."

The officer lowered his arm but stayed firmly in Andy's path. "Where were you just now, sir?"

Andy stared at him. "On the beach. I couldn't sleep, so I went for a walk."

"Can anyone corroborate that?" the officer asked.

Andy stiffened. "I was alone. Didn't pass anyone. I can show you my footprints."

"Officer, please." Helicity edged around the man to stand next to her brother. "He has trouble sleeping sometimes. We both do." She laced her fingers through Andy's and gave the policeman the abbreviated version of what they'd been through in Michigan as well as that afternoon's distressing events. Andy showed him his bandage as proof of his latest injury.

The officer relaxed his stance somewhat. "I'm sorry. But I had to ask. It's my job."

Andy gave him a curt nod, then turned to Helicity.

"What happened here?" When she repeated the same story she'd told the police, his grip on her hand tightened. "God. You must have been terrified. And you didn't see the guy's face?"

She shook her head. "It was too dark, and his hoodie was up." She shivered. "And he was in and out of here so fast."

The officer cut in. "We know he took whatever cash he could get his hands on," he said with a nod at the empty tip jar and Suze's splayed-open wallet. "Oddly enough, he didn't take the credit cards. And what would he have grabbed off the living room table?"

"I don't know," Helicity said. "I couldn't see it. I just know it was something small enough to stuff in his pocket."

Suze's eyes widened. "Wait. Mia's pills. I left the bottle there. I just remembered."

"Pills?" The officer scowled. "What kind of pills?"

Suze scrubbed her face with her hands. "Prescription painkillers. The narcotic kind."

"Opioids." The officer's lips tightened further. "Right. I'm going to need a list of everybody who would have known about those pills."

"What? Why?" Andy asked.

The policeman narrowed his eyes. "Because whoever broke in seemed to know what he was after. Targeted the pills and the cash and nothing else."

"I can give you the list," Suze said. "But can we let these kids get back to bed, please?"

The officer hesitated, then nodded. Suze led him through the back door onto the deck. Someone had swept up the broken glass and taped a square of cardboard over the windowpane. Helicity shivered again, remembering the intruder standing in the doorway. Then she rounded on Andy and searched his face with her eyes.

"Were you really by yourself? Or were you with Johnny?"

His grasp on her hand loosened and he turned away. "I'm not in the habit of lying to the police, Hel."

She stared at his back. She wanted to believe him. But that little voice in her head wouldn't let her.

Nobody tells anyone everything.

Suddenly, the energy drained out of her, and she sagged against the kitchen island. Sam made a move toward her, but Mia was quicker. "Come on, Hel," she whispered, guiding her toward the loft stairs. "Bedtime."

Sleep cradled Helicity in its arms soon after her head hit the pillow. But in the hours just before dawn, a new nightmare invaded her slumber.

She was adrift on a boat far out on a fog-thick sea. Something was out there with her. Something she didn't want to see. Something she knew she couldn't avoid.

The mist parted, and she spied a figure struggling in the waves. Invisible forces propelled her closer. Crying for help, the figure thrashed in the clutches of some unseen creature hell-bent on dragging him below the surface. She stretched out her arms, beseeching him to reach for her. To trust her.

But to her horror, he pulled away and gave himself up to the beast below. She locked gazes with him just before he slipped beneath the surface. His eyes were the same sea-green color as her own . . . before the monster turned them zombie-undead.

Helicity awoke in a slick of sweat and with a scream lodged in her throat. The scream had a name: *Andy.*

CHAPTER NINETEEN

"I'm sorry, Helicity. Andy's gone."

After her nightmare, Helicity had fallen into a mercifully dreamless sleep. Mia was already up and in the shower when she finally awoke. She headed downstairs, hoping—expecting—to see Andy.

Now she stared at Suze uncomprehendingly. "What? When?"

Suze pulled a fresh-baked coffee cake from the oven, filling the air with the rich scent of cinnamon and brown sugar, reminding Helicity that a family of guests was due to arrive later that day. "Andy left with his friend Johnny a while ago. I told him he should take the day off, but he was determined to go."

Helicity leaned forward on the kitchen island, covered her face with her hands, and then pushed her fingers through her hair. Her talk with Andy would have to wait. Again.

Sam was gone, too, though he texted her to say he'd be back for their visit with Trey. Where he was or what he was doing, he didn't mention.

Helicity and Suze spent the rest of the morning vacuuming, dusting, and tidying the Beachside for the new guests. Mia helped with lighter duties that didn't aggravate her bruised back. A man replaced the broken glass and repaired the damaged motion detectors. By the time Sam returned to take them to visit Trey, all evidence of the burglary was gone.

Helicity hoped her nightmares would vanish as cleanly.

Trey's house was similar in style to Suze's, except the outside was shingled with weathered gray boards rather than painted turquoise, and there were regular windows rather than huge picture windows facing the Gulf. Trey was in the living room, his injured leg propped up on the floral-patterned sofa. Mia sat in one chair facing him and Sam took another, leaving Helicity no choice but to sit beside Trey's feet.

Mia immediately filled Trey in on the break-in. Trey's mouth formed a horrified O when she finished. "You're lucky he didn't see you!" he said to Helicity.

She shook her head. "I keep thinking I should have gone for my phone sooner. Then maybe the police would have caught him in the act."

"No," Trey objected. "You were smart not to try to stop him. From what I've heard, drug addicts will do anything to feed their habit. *Anything.*" He gave the word a dark emphasis.

"Drug addicts?" Mia shivered. "You think this guy was one?"

"Makes sense, doesn't it? He steals your pills and the cash, but not any of Suze's stuff." Then he gave a sheepish grin. "Also, the police think drugs are behind all those robberies. Said so on the news this morning."

"You watch the news?" Mia joked.

"For the sports," Trey said defensively. "Plus, my hospital roommate wanted to watch it. Oh, and guess who was interviewed." He rolled his eyes. "Summer. Some reporter found out she'd been in the derecho.

She made it sound like she'd saved us single-handedly."

They all gave a collective groan. While the skier's assessment of Summer as a "waste" had struck Helicity as a little harsh, she had no patience for that kind of shallow, self-centered person. From the disgusted looks on her friends' faces, they felt the same way.

Sam cleared his throat. "Speaking of saving . . . I owe you, Trey. Big-time."

Trey held up his hands. "You got me off that sailboat, man. We're even."

"Not in my book." Sam stood up, withdrew a slightly crumpled envelope from his pocket, and handed it to Trey. "I got you this to say thanks."

Looking mystified, Trey opened it and withdrew a letter. His eyes scanned the contents, then his face broke into a wide grin. "It's an open invitation from the marine mammal rehab center to visit Scar!"

"Scar?" Mia queried.

"That's the name they gave the dolphin," Trey said, "because of the white scar on his fin." He waved the paper in the air. "I've been trying to get in ever since that day. How'd you manage it?"

"I went there this morning," Sam replied. "Told

them what you did for me, and how much you'd like to see the other mammal you saved."

"That *Helicity* saved," Trey corrected.

Sam nodded. "Which is why she gets to go with you."

"Can I go, too?" Mia asked. Then her eyes darted between Helicity and Trey. "Oh, shoot. I just remembered I'm busy that day."

"But we haven't said what day we're going," Helicity protested.

"Yeah, but still . . . I'm busy. Probably. So, it'll have to be just you two. Right, Sam?" Mia looked pointedly at Sam.

Sam nodded, his expression impossible to read.

"Just us two." Trey sat forward and caught Helicity's hand. "It's kind of like a date, I guess." His fingers felt warm against hers, and his happy smile spread that warmth throughout the rest of her body.

Mia gave a subtle fist pump that Helicity hoped Trey had missed.

She almost missed something herself. A tightening of Sam's lips. A glimpse of sadness and regret quickly hidden behind a smile that didn't quite reach his eyes.

"Sam." She gestured to the letter. "You didn't have to do this."

Sam looked away. "Hey, if it weren't for you—for both of you," he said lightly, "I wouldn't be here."

They left Trey's soon after that. Sam dropped Mia and Helicity at the Beachside but didn't get out of the car. "Got to go set up the campsite," he told Helicity. When she offered to help, he smirked. "No offense," he said, revving the engine, "but you're looking a little rough. I'm afraid you'd poke yourself in the eye with one of the poles."

He drove off, leaving her stung by his comment and feeling abandoned for the second time that day. Then her phone rang.

"It's Trey," she told Mia.

Mia grinned. "Yeah, it is." She hurried up the stairs to let Helicity answer the call in private.

"Good news!" Trey said. "Assuming my leg is healing fast, which it will because I am an awesome healer, Mom has agreed to let me visit Scar in two days. So, what do you say, Hel?"

She stared at the impressions left by Sam's wheels, then turned away. "I'd say it's a date."

Suze's guests had arrived while they were at Trey's. The parents, Ted and Lisa Gibson, seemed pleasant enough, if a little bland. Their teenage daughter, Cynthia, had strawberry-blond hair, brown eyes, and a shapely figure that made Helicity feel like a boy by comparison. Her younger brother, Ted Junior, had the same coloring and a talent for annoying his sister. After five minutes of listening to them bicker, Helicity couldn't wait to escape to the beach with Mia.

"Promise me you and Andy will never argue like that," Mia groaned as they spread their towels in the hot sand.

"You have my permission to yell at us if we do," Helicity said. She applied sunscreen and, with a sigh, stretched out on her stomach and closed her eyes. Bathed in the sun and sand's warmth, she felt the chaos of the previous day and night float away. She dozed off almost instantly.

Sam's voice woke her. "So, this your first time on the peninsula?"

"Yeah." There was a throaty chuckle. "And my close friends call me Cyn."

Helicity's eyes flew open. Thirty yards away, Sam

was lounging on his side on a towel with the girl from the Beachside. She was propped on her elbows, her head tipped back and her hair cascading down behind her like a strawberry-blond waterfall. Her teal bikini barely covered her curves.

Sam couldn't take his eyes off her.

"Well, Cyn." Grinning, he got to his feet and held out his hands. "Want to go for a swim?"

With the lazy slowness of a sleepy cat, Cyn smiled. "I'd rather watch you."

Sam cocked an eyebrow. "Well. Then watch away." He turned and strode into the surf.

Until that moment, Helicity didn't think she could hate anyone more than Johnny. But Cyn vaulted into top position. She turned her face away and squeezed her eyes shut. A tear leaked out and traced a line across the bridge of her nose.

Don't you dare cry, she screamed at herself. *He's a friend. Nothing more. Be strong.*

But nothing she'd faced—not the tornado's fury, the flood's power, or the derecho's wildness—had prepared her for that sucker punch to her heart. And gut. She felt sick all over. She had no reason to hate this girl but she felt envy growing by the moment. By the time the darkness of night fell, the green monster of jealousy had overtaken her brain.

That night, she fell asleep clutching Lana's lightning bolt necklace. Sam's photograph lay facedown on her table.

CHAPTER TWENTY

"Three more days of this?" Mia stared daggers at Cyn from the kitchen Friday morning. "I might kill her before Monday checkout."

"Get in line," Suze muttered back. Then she pasted on a smile and offered her guests a fresh cup of coffee.

The Beachside, once a peaceful refuge, had turned into a tension-filled abyss because of Cyn. The girl seemed to take pleasure in making life difficult for Suze, Mia, and Helicity. Wet towels on the bathroom floor and clumps of hair in the shower drain. A browned banana peel and a hardened wad of chewed gum on the bedside table, though the trash bin was just a few feet away. Sand tracked everywhere despite a posted request for guests to brush off their feet before entering.

Added to Helicity's private torture was the fact that Cyn and Sam were glued at the hip every waking moment, from what she could see. Or tried not to see, for the sight of them with their heads close together, laughing and whispering, their hands touching, made her blood turn to ice.

Unfortunately, avoiding Sam meant avoiding the boys' campsite, the only place she was likely to see Andy. Her brother checked in with her via text and phone call now and then, but for all the time they spent together, he might as well have still been in Michigan.

She did manage to escape Thursday afternoon, when she biked to Trey's house and ended up staying for dinner. After the dark cloud of Cyn, the Valdezes were like a breath of fresh air, and she inhaled as much of it as she could. She returned to the Beachside that evening feeling lighter and looking forward to her date with Trey the next afternoon.

A drizzling rain had just started falling when she stowed the bike below the deck and mounted the back stairs. Inside, she found Suze, Mia, and Cyn's parents watching something on television with concerned looks. Cyn was there, too, phone in hand, her bare legs draped over the arm of Suze's favorite chair and her mouth pouting for a selfie.

Helicity skirted past her and sat next to Mia. "What's going on?"

"That tropical depression has grown into a tropical storm," Suze replied grimly. "They're predicting it could turn into a hurricane soon."

"Is it headed this way?" Helicity asked.

"It could be," Suze said cautiously. "We should know more by tomorrow. If it is, they'll issue a hurricane watch." She turned to the Gibsons. "You should know that if the storm does strengthen and enter the Gulf, they will likely order a voluntary evacuation for the peninsula."

"What the hell does that mean?" Cyn demanded.

"Cynthia. Language, please," her mother chided mildly.

"It means residents are strongly urged to leave because it could get dangerous," Suze answered. "Heavy rains, crazy winds, it doesn't take more than a tropical storm to cause serious damage. You do not want to get stranded on the peninsula if a hurricane, even a weak one, comes near here. My suggestion? If there's even a chance this storm comes near us, leave sooner than later. We will, too. We've seen the worst down here."

That made everyone, even Cyn, fall silent. Then Cyn's father slapped his knees and stood up. "Well, we'll just have to hope it doesn't come this way, because I'd hate to cut our time here short! Now, how about we watch a movie instead of the weather?"

Helicity and Mia made their excuses midway through the opening credits. "What do you think?" Mia asked as they flopped onto their beds. "Are we in for a hurricane?"

"Whether it strengthens from a tropical storm to a hurricane depends on a lot of things," Helicity said. "Enough warm, moist air to fuel the storm system, the way and strength of the wind in the upper atmosphere—"

"No, I meant, are *we* in for a hurricane? As in us, right here?" Mia's voice had an edge to it.

She's scared, Helicity thought suddenly. After the derecho, she couldn't blame her. Even with her own fascination with the weather, the thought of being caught in another storm was making her uneasy, too. But that wasn't what Mia needed to hear.

"Listen, tropical storms fizzle out all the time. But if this one doesn't, you can bet we'll be out of here in plenty of time. So, there's nothing to worry about."

Mia visibly relaxed. "I know I sometimes make fun of your weather obsession, Hel. But right now, I'm glad you know about this stuff."

Thursday night's light rain gave way to a bright, beautiful Friday without a cloud in the sky. Helicity checked the storm first thing that morning and was able to deliver the happy report to Mia that while it was still aiming toward the Gulf, it hadn't strengthened beyond a tropical storm.

"Too bad," Mia said jokingly. "A hurricane watch might have ejected Cyn's family a day or two sooner."

"Hey. Look on the bright side. The storm could power up again."

"Ah. We can only hope." Mia paused. "Forget I said that."

"Done."

Helicity whipped through her chores as quickly as she could that morning. She ate a quick lunch, then showered and got ready for her date with Trey.

At least, she thought she was ready until Mia gave her T-shirt and shorts a disapproval rating of *Ugh*. "Not cute enough," she objected.

She pawed through Helicity's clothing and chose a seafoam-green dress with a fitted top and wide straps that crisscrossed in back. Below the waist, the short skirt flared in soft folds. "This," she declared.

"Isn't it a little . . . formal?" Helicity said doubtfully. Her mother had insisted she pack the dress in case she went out to a nice dinner.

Mia thrust the dress at her stubbornly. "This. Now. And these." She scooped up a pair of tan strappy flats. "Add your dolphin earrings and a brush of mascara, and you're good to go."

"I'll wear the earrings because I love them. But you can forget the mascara."

"It's not like you need it anyway," Mia groused. "Not with those long lashes of yours."

Laughing, Helicity quickly changed into the dress,

combed her hair, added the earrings and sandals, then turned to face Mia. "Okay?"

Mia smiled. "Better than okay. Look." She spun Helicity to the full-length mirror.

Helicity blinked when she saw her reflection. She'd never cared much about clothes, preferring to wear whatever was most comfortable or fit the task of the day. Oversize T-shirts handed down from Andy, shorts, flannel shirts, hoodies, and jeans—those made up the bulk of her wardrobe.

Now for the first time, she understood that the right outfit could make you feel special. Confident, even. The color of the dress turned her eyes a more brilliant shade of green. The top hugged her without being tight and the skirt flowed with her movements. The silver earrings added just the right amount of shimmer. Her hair swept her bare shoulders, the tawny locks matching her skin's honey-gold tan. The small nicks and bruises she'd suffered during the derecho were exposed, but somehow, those imperfections made her look real.

"Wait. One last thing." Helicity snagged Lana's necklace from her table and looped it over her head.

Mia nodded with satisfaction. "Trey's not going to know what hit him."

If so, he wasn't the only one. Sam looked thunderstruck by her appearance when Helicity descended the loft stairs. "Fifteen." It came out hoarsely. He cleared his throat and tried again. "Fifteen. You look . . . different."

It was the most he'd said to her in the last day and a half. She swallowed her hurt and replied, "Just on the outside. On the inside, I'm still me."

"Sammy? You coming?" Cyn called from the deck.

Sam hesitated, eyes still on Helicity. Then Helicity's phone buzzed. She took it out of the tiny purse Mia had loaned her. The dolphin statue selfie appeared with a message that Trey and his mother were pulling into the parking area.

Seeing the picture seemed to shake Sam loose. "Yeah. I'm coming." To Helicity, he said, "Have fun. You deserve it. You, and Trey."

CHAPTER TWENTY-ONE

Trey met Helicity at the bottom of the stairs. When she saw him squirming in a collared golf shirt and nice shorts, she silently thanked Mia for insisting on the dress.

Mrs. Valdez dropped them off at the ferry. On board, they found empty seats on the upper deck. Trey sat down with a grimace.

"Does your leg hurt?" Helicity asked anxiously. "If you need to head back or—"

"Not a chance," Trey responded. "I've been looking forward to this for two days."

Helicity smiled. "Me too."

"I have a confession." Trey leaned his elbows on his thighs and swiveled his head to look up at her. "I, um . . . I've never been on a date before." His expression and his voice had an uncertain quality that made her heart melt just a little bit.

"Me neither. Mia had to pick out my outfit for me."

Trey burst out laughing. "My dad told me what to wear. And tell Mia she did a great job. You look awesome."

"So do you."

The ferry docked in Galveston twenty minutes later. Helicity offered her hand to help Trey to his feet. He took it. And held it as they disembarked.

Sam had arranged for a volunteer from the marine mammal rehab center to meet them in the ferry parking lot. It turned out to be the same woman who had spoken to them on the beach when Scar was rescued. AMANDA, the name embroidered on her bright red volunteer uniform read. She greeted them sincerely, then filled them in on Scar's condition as she drove them to the center.

"Near as we can tell," she said, "Scar beached

himself while chasing after fish. Dolphins do that sometimes—herd a school toward shore to trap them, then end up getting trapped themselves. Lucky it was just one dolphin and not a whole pod. And that he didn't strand because of disease or . . ."

"Or what?" Helicity begged.

"Or chemicals leaching into the water, oil spills in the Gulf. Man-made disasters. When a dolphin—or any sea creature—is exposed to something toxic like that . . . well, it's not something you want any living thing to suffer through." Amanda was quiet for a moment, then smiled. "But, like I said, we think Scar was just a little overzealous in his hunt for food. He's doing great. In fact, he's scheduled for release early next week."

They pulled into the rehab center parking lot. It was more than one building, Helicity saw; actually an industrial-looking complex she could have walked right by without guessing its true purpose. Amanda led them to the nearest building and opened the door. Inside was a desk littered with paperwork, a few display cases containing animal skulls and bones, and a huge wall map of the Gulf. The air was redolent with the smell of fish mixed with a rank, low-tide odor.

"Phew!" Trey wrinkled his nose.

Amanda chuckled. "Yeah, that takes some getting used to. But it's worth it for this." She ushered them through another door.

Helicity stopped short in amazement. Inside this section of the building was an enormous rectangular in-ground pool. The ceiling was two stories above them, giving the space an open, airy feel. At the far end of the pool was a large platform partially submerged in the water. And swimming in the water was Scar.

The last time she'd seen him, he'd been immobilized on a stretcher. Now, like a sleek gray torpedo, he skimmed just below the surface of the water, surging forward with powerful strokes of his flukes. As Helicity drew near, the top of his head broke the water's plane, and his blowhole opened and closed with quick gasps of breath. Then he dipped below again, his dorsal fin with its distinctive white slash slicing through the waves.

"Oh," Helicity breathed. "He's so beautiful."

Amanda gestured toward the dolphin. "Go ahead. You can get closer."

Helicity didn't need another invitation. She moved to the pool's edge and knelt. The hem of her dress dipped into a puddle, and her sandals were instantly soaked. But she didn't care. Just a glimpse of Scar's natural smile was enough to make her grin like an idiot.

Trey sank down beside her, equally captivated. "Best first date ever," he murmured.

Amanda produced a bin with pool toys—a nubbly playground ball, a weighted rubber ring, a bunch of foam noodles, and more. "These are EEDs, or environmental enrichment devices," she told them as she tossed a few into the water.

"Why does a dolphin need toys?" Trey asked.

"Dolphins are incredibly intelligent animals," Amanda said. "He'd get bored with nothing to do. These devices provide stimulation."

Helicity watched fascinated as Scar mouthed the floating ball and then pushed it around with his snout. He seemed to play a game with the ring next, scooping it up, putting it down and swimming away, and then scooping it up again. With Amanda's permission, Helicity videoed Scar for a few minutes before slipping her phone back into Mia's purse. She wanted something to remind her of the day, but she wanted to truly experience it—without a screen in the way— even more.

They stayed at the pool for more than an hour. To Helicity it felt like ten minutes. She realized this was the happiest, most peaceful, and free of anxiety she had been in a long time. She glanced at Trey.

Calm. Relaxed. That's how he makes me feel.

And without meaning to compare, the image of Sam entered as the perfect antithesis. Sam always brought up some anxiety, but excitement and mystery, too.

Amanda interrupted her inadvertent checklist comparison when she reluctantly informed them that it was time to go. Helicity was about to stand when Scar drifted over with the ring in his mouth. She held her breath as he rolled to his side and looked up at her with his liquid black eye.

"Do you remember me?" she whispered, her voice no louder than the beat of a moth's wing. She wanted to believe it. To believe that the connection she felt with Scar wasn't one-way. That when he was released into the wild next week, he would take a memory of her with him, just as she had her video.

Scar regarded her for another long moment. Then he took a quick breath and dove below the surface with his toy.

Amanda spent another hour with Trey and Helicity, showing them the complex's research facility, education center, and other tanks that housed sea life in various stages of recovery. At one point, Helicity asked something that had been on her mind since Amanda first told them about the problems with chemicals and oil.

"You mentioned man-made disasters earlier. What about natural disasters? What do dolphins do during a hurricane?"

Amanda raised her eyebrows. "Interesting question. Nobody knows because no one has ever studied their behavior in the midst of such a destructive storm. The accepted theory is that the heavy rains that precede the storm change the salinity—that's the salt level—in the seawater. The dolphins sense that change and flee to deeper, safer waters. Whether that's true or not . . ." She shrugged.

The tour ended shortly after that. "By the way," Amanda mentioned as they walked back to the main entrance, "most of the people who work here are volunteers. In another year or two, when you're sixteen, you can both go through the training program, if you like."

"I wish I could," Helicity replied with regret, "but I don't actually live here. In fact, I'm returning to Michigan sometime in the next few weeks. Before school starts."

Trey suddenly stumbled. Helicity caught his arm to keep him from falling. "Whoa! You all right?"

"My leg," he muttered. "It's starting to ache. Okay with you if we head out?"

"Of course!"

Amanda drove them back to the ferry. "Hope you feel better, Trey. And keep an eye on our Facebook page for updates on Scar's release."

Helicity and Trey thanked her profusely, then boarded. Trey limped up the metal stairs to the top deck and collapsed on a bench with a groan. His expression was tight with pain and his face was coated with a sheen of sweat.

"Oh, my God, Trey!" Alarmed, Helicity sat down, twisting to face him. "You're really hurting! Why didn't you say something sooner?"

He offered her a smile. "And ruin our day? Not a chance. Especially since we don't have a whole lot more of them ahead of us. See, I kind of forgot you were leaving Bolivar."

"Not right away."

"Yeah. Anyway." He tipped his head back and closed his eyes. "I'll be fine."

Helicity found herself studying Trey's face. In all the time they'd spent together, she'd never had a chance to look at him that closely. Now her eyes traveled over his soft curls and dark lashes. Traced the chiseled contours of his cheeks and chin. Took in the faint shadow of mustache above his upper lip. Then zeroed in on the lips themselves.

I could kiss him.

The thought caught her off guard. Flustered, she started to turn away when the ferry blasted its horn to signal the start of its journey. Trey's eyes suddenly opened. His warm brown gaze captured her, rooting her in place.

"Hey," he whispered, not moving.

"Hey," she whispered back, heart thumping. She was dimly aware of footsteps behind her. Whose, she didn't know or care.

Then Trey's gaze shifted. A slight frown creased his forehead. "What are you doing here?"

Helicity glanced over her shoulder. And gulped. *"Sam?"*

Sam wore an expression like thunder. "Fifteen," he growled. "Don't you ever check your phone?"

The wallpaper on Helicity's lock screen was all but hidden beneath a lengthy list of missed texts and phone calls. All of them were from Sam—except one.

> LANA'S AWAKE! CALL ASAP!

The text was from Ray, Lana's longtime storm-chasing partner. Helicity leaped up from the bench and stared at Sam, not daring to believe the words. "She's awake?"

Sam broke into a broad grin. "She's awake, Fifteen.

I talked to Ray half an hour ago. She's awake, and she's asking for you. For us."

For a split second, Helicity was too overcome to react. Then she hurled herself into Sam's arms. Laughing, he wrapped her in a crushing embrace. She'd been hugged countless times in her life, by Andy, her parents, Mia, and others. But none had felt as powerful—as *right*— as this one. She wanted it to go on forever.

"So what do you think?" Sam said, dropping his arms but still standing close. "Time to head home?"

"Yes!" she said with a joyful laugh.

"No!"

Trey's cry startled Helicity. She'd been so caught up in her excitement that she'd momentarily forgotten he was there. But now she saw the hurt in his eyes. "I mean, what's the big rush?" he asked.

Helicity bit her lip. "You don't understand. Lana . . . she saved my life and ever since . . . Trey, I never even got to thank her!" She eased down next to him. "I'm sure we won't be leaving for a few days yet, but the sooner we can get back to see her, to make sure she's really okay, the better."

Trey's face fell, but he nodded. "Yeah. I guess

that's more important than anything . . . or anyone . . . down here."

Helicity didn't reply. Denying it would have been a lie; agreeing would have meant hurting Trey's feelings more than she already had. She liked him far too much to do that.

The ferry docked in Bolivar a few minutes later. Sam had left his car at the far end of the ferry parking lot. He hurried over to it. "You coming, Fifteen?"

"Helicity! Trey! Over here!" Mrs. Valdez had pulled up close to save Trey the extra steps. Now she was waving to them from her car window.

Helicity looked uncertainly from one vehicle to the other.

"Go on," Trey finally said.

"I'll call you later," Helicity promised. Then on impulse, she raised up on her tiptoes and kissed Trey on the cheek. "I'm so glad you were my first date," she whispered.

"I wish we had time for more," Trey answered. Then he smiled, and his usual sunny disposition shone its warmth on her. "But hey, you're not gone yet. And there's always texts and Facebook, right?"

Helicity smiled back. Then she made her way to where Sam was waiting.

"All good?" Sam asked casually as she slid into the seat beside him.

"Good enough," she answered.

He shot her a quick look but didn't ask anything more. Instead, he started the car and headed out onto the main road. When Sam learned she hadn't had dinner, he drove through a local burger joint. She tried to give him her last ten dollars to pay for the meal, but he waved it off and parked in a spot so she could eat without being jostled about.

As she munched on her fries, something occurred to her. "Andy! Does he know?"

Sam gave a snort of laughter. "I texted him a bunch of times, but you Dunlaps must have a genetic defect about texting back because he hasn't replied."

"I'll try calling him." Helicity licked her fingers clean, pulled out her phone, and thumbed her way to Andy's phone number. When Andy's phone went to voice mail, she hung up, intending to text him instead. Then Sam held up a finger.

"Wait. Try him again. Then listen."

When Helicity redialed, she didn't hear anything at first. Then her ears picked up a faint chirping. "That's the ring tone Andy assigned me." She couldn't locate the source before the sound stopped. Then something Andy had said in the hospital a few days ago came back to her. "Hold on. Is his duffel bag in the trunk?"

"He usually tosses it there before heading to work, so it should be."

"I bet he left his phone inside it. Can you pop the trunk?" She redialed Andy's number again and climbed out of the car. In the trunk, Andy's duffel bag sat in a rumpled lump on top of the camping gear, the phone inside chirping away like a trapped bird. Rolling her eyes, Helicity unzipped the zipper.

"Ugh!"

The ripe odor of unwashed clothes made her reluctant to touch anything, but she poked at the pile with a finger. She hit something hard. His phone, she assumed, until she pushed aside a dirty sock and found his orange pill bottle lying beneath it. A handful of pills rested inside the plastic container. She was about to keep searching when the name on the bottle's label leaped out at her. It wasn't Andy's name.

It was Mia's.

She stared at it uncomprehendingly. *How did Mia's pill bottle get in Andy's duffel bag?*

"Did you find it?"

Helicity jumped. Sam was out of the car and coming around to the back. Quick as lightning and without thinking why, she snatched up the bottle and hid it in her cupped hand as she yanked the zipper closed.

"No," she replied with false cheeriness. "It's buried in his bag with some really nasty laundry. I'll make Andy dig it out himself. But since he doesn't have his phone," she added as an idea struck her, "maybe we could track him down at that house he's painting."

Sam nodded. "Worth a shot."

Helicity slipped the pill bottle into her purse when Sam wasn't looking. She was still trying to understand how it had gotten into Andy's bag when they pulled up in front of an older house. Unlike newer construction, this one was raised only a few feet from the ground. A thickset man in a paint-speckled T-shirt, shorts, and baseball cap was loading equipment—ladders, buckets, brushes, and tarps—into the back of a van.

"Help you with something?" he drawled when Helicity and Sam approached.

"We're looking for Andy," Helicity replied. "Is he around?"

"No Andy here." The man tipped back his hat and scratched his head. "Unless you mean Drew?"

Helicity grimaced at the name. "Yes. Drew. Is he here?"

"Not since Monday, no. Had to let him go for slacking off. That, and he tracked white footprints on the deck."

Helicity blinked. "But . . . he fell off a ladder here on Tuesday."

The man snorted. "Not here he didn't. And not likely at any other paint job, either. Word gets around about bad workers, see." He narrowed his eyes. "Why you so interested in finding him, anyway? He owe you money, too?"

"Owe me money?" Helicity repeated faintly.

The man shrugged. "None of my business, of course, but I overheard him telling that guy who gives him rides not to worry, that he'd come up with the cash."

"That guy." Helicity swallowed hard. The burger and fries felt like lead weights in her stomach. "What did he look like?"

"Blond. Skinny. Wore a necklace with beads on it."

"Not beads," Sam said grimly. "Shark teeth." He looked at Helicity. "Johnny."

She nodded, not trusting herself to speak. Sam had one more question, though. "Do you give your workers cell phones?"

The man looked at him like he was crazy. "Oh, you mean in case there's a big paint emergency or something?" he scoffed.

Back in the car, Helicity stared blankly out the windshield. Her mind was spinning.

All her life, she had felt a bond with her brother, a trust and love that no one and nothing could ever shatter. But now his lies—about his phone, his fall, his job—had cracked that bond.

Nobody tells anyone everything, Sam had warned her.

What else has he been hiding from me?

She knew the answer even before she asked herself the question. Like land mines waiting to explode, the evidence was all there. His erratic moods. His disturbed sleep. His friendship with Johnny. His abrupt departure from Michigan. Odd moments back home that she had dismissed or taken little notice of, but that now, looking back, took on significance. And the biggest land mine . . . the orange pill bottle burning a hole in her purse.

Sam climbed into the driver's seat, breaking into her thoughts. "Listen," he said as he started the car and pulled onto the road, "I'm sure there's a perfectly good explanation for all . . . this." He whirled a hand in the air.

Helicity clutched Lana's necklace, needing to feel the certainty of its solidness, the sharpness of its jagged edges. "There *is* an explanation." Her voice was raw. "But it's not a good one. In fact, it's bad. It's really, really bad."

She withdrew the bottle and stared at the little white pills inside.

"I think . . . I think Andy stole Mia's painkillers. And our money. And I think he did it because he's addicted."

am yanked the steering wheel to the side, braked to a hard stop on the road's shoulder, and switched off the engine. *"What?"*

Wordlessly, Helicity handed him the bottle. As he scanned the label, his expression morphed from disbelief to confusion to understanding and, finally, to anger.

"Idiot! Complete, total idiot!" He swore and hurled the bottle against the dashboard. It ricocheted back onto the seat and bounced to the floor, the pills rattling inside the orange plastic like a maraca.

"I know," Helicity said tearfully. "Andy—"

"Not Andy," Sam interrupted. "Me. For not realizing it sooner. It's all so obvious now, isn't it? The way he's been acting, how he's been avoiding you—everything."

Helicity said nothing. Not because she thought Sam should have known what was going on, but because she blamed herself for ignoring what was right in front of her.

They sat in silence, the ticking of the engine and the occasional car speeding by the only sounds. Sam restarted the car when the sun threatened to turn the interior into a sauna. The pill bottle rolled as they moved onto the road. For one brief moment, Helicity thought about crushing it beneath her foot. Destroying the evidence and forgetting she'd ever seen it. Instead, she picked it up and returned it to her purse. When Sam shot her a questioning look, she murmured, "I have to confront him with it. Otherwise, he'll just lie to me again."

"And what about Suze and Mia? Will you show it to them, too? Or tell your parents?"

Tears pricked Helicity's eyes at the thought of

what they might say or do. "I know I should. But I want to see Andy first. Give him a chance to explain."

Sam's mouth tightened into a thin line of disagreement, but he nodded.

They drove in silence straight to the campsite. If Andy was going to show up anywhere, it would be there.

The sunlight had faded by the time they got the tents up, but Andy still hadn't appeared. Helicity sat on the beach, digging her toes into the warm sand and listening to the *shush* of the waves. Her purse, its contents like a ticking time bomb, was in the sand beside her. She tried to imagine the conversation she would have with Andy about the painkillers. About everything. But it was impossible. Such a conversation was uncharted territory where her mind refused to go.

"Hey." Sam sat down beside her. "I should take you back to the Beachside. Mia and Suze are probably wondering where you are. You can do Andy's laundry, use it as a reason to come back here later."

A few minutes later and with Andy's duffel over her shoulder, Helicity made her way up the stairs to the Beachside kitchen. She expected Mia to bombard her with questions about her date with Trey the moment she walked through the door.

Instead, she found her friend hunched over her half-eaten dinner at the kitchen island, talking to Suze in low, tense tones. For one heart-stopping moment, she thought they'd learned the truth about Andy and the break-in. "Everything all right?" she asked tentatively.

Suze straightened. "We just heard that the tropical storm has strengthened to a hurricane. A Cat-2. They're predicting it will grow even stronger in the next twenty-four hours."

Helicity knew tropical storms could amass great power in a short period of time, given the right conditions. Still, she was shocked that this one had grown so strong so quickly.

"Do the computer models have it tracking this way?"

Hurricane forecasters typically generated two types of models. Most people see the displays as colorful spaghetti plots on TV. Those spaghetti plots followed the dozens of computer models produced by gathering all available data—from satellites, dropsondes lowered into the storm by hurricane hunters—to diagram the different paths a storm might take. The ends of the strings were joined together at the storm's current location, then squiggled apart like spaghetti strands to show each possible track. The second model, known as the cone of probability, was the National Hurricane Center's official storm scenario. It plotted the hurricane's most likely position and strength at intervals ranging from 24 to 120 hours in the future. Everyone living within the cone was warned of the storm's potential impact.

Mia nodded grimly. "Most of the models have the hurricane coming here. Maybe even as soon as tomorrow night." She lowered her eyes and traced a vein in the island's granite surface. "Lucky for me, I'll be home by then."

Helicity startled. "What?"

Mia looked up. "After the derecho, I called my mom. Not just to tell her I was okay. To tell her I wanted to come home. So . . . she booked me a ticket. I was supposed to leave Monday but now I fly out tomorrow morning."

"Oh."

"Don't hate me, Hel," Mia said miserably. "I already

feel like I'm abandoning you. But the truth is, I'm glad to be going. With the derecho, and now this hurricane—Hel, I'm not like you. The thought of being caught in another storm makes me want to throw up."

"No, no! It's totally okay," Helicity hastened to assure her, "because I have some news, too." She quickly filled her in on Lana's status and the plan to head home. "It sounds like we'll all be getting out in the nick of time."

"Speaking of getting out," Suze put in, "tell Sam and Andy to crash here for the night. The beach is no place to camp out with a major storm looming. And I could use their help boarding up the windows. Just as a precaution," she added with a reassuring glance at Mia. Helicity imagined how prone the Beachside had to be to hurricane damage. How scared Suze must be, since the Beachside was not just her moneymaker, but her home.

Helicity promised to tell the boys, then carried Andy's duffel bag to the laundry room. As she was halfway through feeding the dirty clothes into the washer, his phone clattered to the floor. She picked it up when the washer was going, flipping it around in her hands and arguing with herself about whether or not to spy on its contents.

The need for information won out. What she hoped to find, she didn't know. But accessing Andy's phone seemed the best, and maybe the only, way of discovering something that might help her understand what he'd been up to, if not why. So, when the black screen sprang to life under her thumb, she swallowed her guilt and took her best guess at his password: *Brady12,* the last name and uniform number of his favorite quarterback.

It worked. *Wow, is he predictable. That was way too easy.* The tiny screen flooded with messages and texts—from her, from Sam, from their parents. She scanned through them, and through his phone log and contact list, too. She noted with dismay that Andy hadn't been returning their parents' calls. There were no communications from Johnny, which confirmed her theory that that's what Andy's other phone was for. Unfortunately, nothing on his family phone hinted at where he might be, what he might be doing, or whom he might be doing it with.

As a last resort, she checked his photo cache. At first glance, it seemed just as useless. Then she spotted a bizarre picture of an old rusty-looking doorway sealed with an equally rusted padlock.

What the heck? She zoomed in. The door was nothing special, just a dinged-up slab of wood or metal with an X-shaped reinforcement riveted to the front. Why would he have taken a pic of that?

After studying it a few moments, she concluded the doorway was most likely located somewhere at Fort Travis, an old military fortification near the ferry terminal. Originally built to safeguard the entrance to Galveston Harbor, the fort and surrounding land was now a public park, though many of the concrete buildings had fallen into disrepair and were blocked off for safety reasons. When Helicity learned that Bolivar residents had sheltered there during Hurricane Carla in 1961, she convinced Trey, Sam, and Mia to roam around the low hillsides, grassy expanses, and dilapidated buildings one afternoon.

She didn't remember seeing Andy's doorway at the fort. All she knew was that it had to have some meaning for him to photograph it. So she texted it to her own phone. Then she slipped both devices into her purse with the pill bottle.

As she came out of the laundry room, she heard new voices. The Gibsons, she realized. She grimaced when she recognized the loudest voice as Cyn's—the last person she wanted to see just then.

In the kitchen, Mia was pretending to be engrossed in a magazine. "They're leaving tonight!" she whispered gleefully. "And I'm ninety-nine percent sure Cyn's talking to Sam. I mean, Sammy." Mia rolled her eyes and smiled at the same time.

Cyn was on her cell on the deck, but the girls could hear every word. "Why did you ditch me for that immature little girl this afternoon?" she yelled in outrage.

"She means you," Mia reported.

"Yeah. I got that. Shh."

Whatever Sam said next turned Cyn's face ugly. "Well, excuse me," she snarled. "I didn't realize she was so important."

Mia raised her eyebrows at Helicity. "What's this now?"

Helicity flushed, then excused herself to change

out of her dress. Downstairs, Cyn's bedroom door slammed shut so hard, Suze's knickknacks trembled.

Helicity's phone buzzed as she was tugging a T-shirt over her head. It was a text from Sam. Before she opened the message to read it, she had a pang of guilt. She shouldn't feel this way about two guys. Not at the same time. Why was she so happy to hear Cyn yelling at Sam? Why was she so pumped to see Sam's name immediately pop up on her phone? She fought off the feeling of "winning" that was consuming her, and when she touched her finger to the home button and the message revealed itself, guilt turned to anguish.

> Andy's here. Better come.

Before she could respond, a second message appeared. Just a single word that crackled with urgency:

> Hurry.

She grabbed her purse and ran.

CHAPTER TWENTY-FOUR

Mia and Suze stared at Helicity in surprise when she dashed down the stairs. "Gotta help Sam with something!" she called as she hurried out the deck door.

The headlights from Sam's car shone like a beacon as she raced down the beach to the campsite. She could hear someone yelling angrily. It took her a moment to recognize the person shouting was Andy. His voice was shrill and downright frightening.

Her brother stood nose to nose with Sam, his hands

balled into fists. "For the last time, Levesque, where's my stuff?"

"Andy!" Helicity cried. "Back off! I have your bag!"

Her brother rounded on her. The harsh lights from the car shadowed his face into a demonic mask of fury. "Well, where is it? Because I need something in it."

Something inside her snapped. She yanked the pill bottle from her purse and flung it at his feet. "Is this what you're looking for? What you *need*?"

Andy flinched as if she'd struck him. "What—is that Mia's— Where'd that come from?" he stammered.

Helicity scowled. "You know where. Your duffel."

"My duffel? No. Someone—someone must have put it there." He spun and stabbed a finger at Sam. "Him! I bet he stole it and planted it in my stuff. I warned you he was no good, Hel. And now you've got proof!"

"What about getting fired from your painting job, Andy?" she spat. "Is Sam responsible for that, too? And for your unexplained late nights? Is he the reason you've been cutting yourself off from Mom and Dad? Why you've avoided me to hang out with that dirtbag Johnny?"

She retrieved the bottle and held it up pinched between her fingers. The orange plastic glowed like an ember in the headlights. "Because I think what's inside this container is the real reason for all that. And maybe more."

She wanted him to deny it. To tell her she was wrong, that it was all a big mistake. To give her an explanation that made sense of everything.

Instead, he gave her a pleading, desperate look that confirmed her worst fears. "Come on, Hel. It's not what you think."

"Isn't it?" With a fierce twist, she opened the bottle and tipped the pills into her palm.

Andy licked his lips. "What are you going to do with those?"

"What I wish you had done with the first pills that doctor in Michigan gave you. And all the others you bought or stole or tricked someone into giving you." Before he could stop her, she ran to the water's edge and hurled the pills far out into the surf.

"*No!*"

Andy's scream pierced the air. He lunged toward the water. Sam moved to intercept, but he was no match for Andy's strength or his years as a football player. Andy tossed him aside like a rag doll, then dropped to his knees in the water.

"Why did you do that, Hel?" Andy rocked back and forth, hugging himself. "You have no idea what I'm going to go through. No idea."

All the fight drained from Helicity then. She dropped the bottle and lowered herself beside him. Pried his arms free and gripped his hands in hers. And looked directly into his eyes for the first time in months. They were so full of fear and hunger and self-loathing that she almost couldn't see what else was hidden there: her brother's true essence, reaching out and crying for help. Just as it had in her nightmare. Except this was reality—and unlike her dream self, she would never let the monster drag him under without a fight.

"You're right," she whispered fiercely. "I don't know what you're going to go through, or where you've been. But I know where you are right now, and that's here with me."

She tightened her grip. He looked so agitated that she wanted to tell him that she understood. That he was going to be all right. But she couldn't bring herself to say the words. There had been too many lies between them already.

Instead, she tried to reach that part of him that was still *him*. "Talk to me, Andy. Please."

Andy stared at her, his mouth working. Then his gaze drifted to the bottle, now washing back and forth in the waves. In that instant, something changed inside him. His face hardened. He pulled his hands from hers and got to his feet. "Hel. I'm sorry. But I have nothing to say that you'd want to hear."

And suddenly, he was running. Not down the beach or into the surf, but to Sam's car. He tore open the driver's-side door, climbed in, and slammed it shut. The locks engaged with a solid *thunk*, and then the engine fired up.

"Andy!" Helicity ran after him, but she was too late. The wheels found purchase, and Andy sped off to the road and disappeared into the night. Defeat and despair robbed her of strength, and she dropped slowly to the sand. "Andy."

"Come on, come on, come on."

She turned at the sound of Sam's muttering. His

thumbs were moving frantically over his phone.

"Who are you calling?"

Sam didn't look up. "My camera."

Helicity's heart dropped. Sam's camera had been mounted to the dashboard of his car. She knew how important it was to him. But still . . . "You're not calling the police, are you?"

"Yes!" He swiped the screen, jabbed a finger at it, and looked up with a triumphant grin. Then he registered her stricken expression and quickly added, "I mean, no, I'm not calling the police! I just remote-started my camera."

At her look of confusion, he flipped his phone around. On the screen was a video of headlights bouncing on a dark roadway. "I didn't have time to explain because the remote-start app has a short range, so I had to fire it up right away, before Andy got too far." He knelt beside her. "The camera automatically uploads video to my phone. As long as he's with the car, we'll be able to see where he's going."

Helicity felt a flash of hope. But then it died. "Won't he realize the camera's on?"

Sam shook his head. "I rigged the dash holder to

cover the view screen so I wouldn't be distracted by the video while driving. You know . . . safety first and all. Now, let's watch."

They leaned their heads together over the phone. For a short time, the video showed side streets lined with weeds and scrub, the occasional electric pole and palm tree, and a few handmade signs advertising local businesses. Then suddenly, the car took a sharp turn. A dilapidated roadside motel with boarded-up windows, cracked pavement, and peeling paint loomed into view. THE HARBORVIEW, a broken marquee read.

Andy parked and turned off the headlights and engine but didn't get out. There was a rustling noise and then Helicity heard Andy's voice. He was on a cell phone, she realized. Not the one their parents paid for. The other one.

"Yeah, it's me." He sounded tense. "Listen, can you meet me at the Harborview?"

He hung up and Helicity and Sam exchanged looks. "Johnny," Sam guessed. Helicity clenched her teeth and nodded.

Not long after the call, another car pulled up. Someone got out and slid in next to Andy.

"Surprised to hear from you, Drew." Johnny's voice made Helicity's blood simmer. "Last time we talked, you said you didn't need anything more from me."

Andy cleared his throat. "I had a supply. But it's gone."

"Uh-huh." Johnny let out a long, disappointed sigh. "Well. That puts you in a tough spot, doesn't it? I mean, I could set you up, obviously. But you already owe me for your last stash. You got cash now?"

Andy started to say something, but Johnny cut him off. "Yeah, I didn't think so. Lucky for you, I got a job that requires a guy with your kind of muscle."

"What kind of job?" Andy asked.

Johnny's low chuckle sent a frisson of dread up Helicity's spine. "Carrying the heavy stuff we're going to steal."

CHAPTER TWENTY-FIVE

H and to her mouth, Helicity listened with growing horror as Johnny outlined his twisted scheme.

"There's a hurricane coming, right? That means people are going to clear off the peninsula. So, we troll the neighborhoods, look for houses being boarded up, people loading their cars, and businesses stupid enough to put 'Closed Due to Storm' signs in their windows. When they move out, we move in." He chuckled again. "But hey, I'm not heartless. We'll make the break-ins look like storm damage, so the owners can claim the insurance. Win-win, right?"

Andy was silent. When he spoke, he sounded as if he was teetering on the edge of despair. "Johnny, I can't—don't make me do this. I'm not a thief."

"Oh, really," Johnny sneered. "You didn't have any trouble helping yourself to some cash a few days ago. Or did that tip jar and wallet empty themselves?"

"I'm going to pay them back! But I'm not going to steal from other people. Besides," Andy added desperately, "getting trapped on the peninsula in a hurricane to rob some houses? That's just insane."

"Is it? Or is it insane not to take advantage of such a golden opportunity?" Johnny's tone turned sly. "But hey, if you really want out, fine. Good luck, though."

"With what?" Andy asked warily.

"Withdrawal." Johnny gave the word a sinister slant. "Heard going cold turkey is a real downer."

A car door opened. Helicity thought Johnny was finally leaving until he added, "Oh, and since you still owe me money . . ."

A close-up of fingers suddenly filled Sam's screen.

"Hey!" Andy cried. "Leave that alone!" The image began tilting and rocking violently.

"Johnny's trying to take the camera!" Helicity cried. "Sam, turn it off before he sees it's on! Hurry!"

Swearing, Sam swiped and stabbed at his phone. The screen went black.

"Do you think Johnny saw it was running?" Helicity asked anxiously. "That he knows someone was listening?"

"Not much we can do about it if he does." Sam was quiet for a moment. Then he added, "But hey, Andy tried to stop him, so that's something, right? And he refused to be Johnny's muscleman or to stick around with the hurricane coming. Since we're his ticket off the peninsula, he'll have to find us before too much longer."

He offered Helicity a hopeful smile, but she just raised and lowered her shoulders. When it came to her brother, she didn't know what to think anymore. She could only hope that the little piece of the old Andy she'd glimpsed would find the strength to come back to her before it was too late.

Until then, sitting in the sand worrying was not an option. "Let's break camp."

After they dismantled the tents, they began moving all the gear to beneath the Beachside deck. Andy didn't return or contact her, but there was nothing she could do about that. She didn't know the number of his burner phone. She didn't know how to track down Johnny, or if Andy was even with him. For all she knew, her brother was driving around the peninsula on his own.

"I'm heading in," she told Sam when the last of the gear was stowed away.

She assumed he would follow her up the stairs then, but he elected to stay by the fire pit so as not to run into Cyn. "I'll watch for headlights at the campsite. If—when—Andy shows up, I'll text you."

But with the winds starting to pick up and a light rain falling, Sam ended up moving indoors to one of Suze's couches. In the morning, he and Helicity discovered his car parked on the beach where the campsite had been. The keys were tucked under the front seat. The camera was inside the glove compartment.

As for Andy, he was nowhere to be found.

* * *

"You're absolutely sure your brother knows about the hurricane?" Suze asked as she fitted a bit into an electric drill. The Gibsons had departed twelve hours later than promised, with a cheery wave from Suze and a muttered "Good riddance" from Mia that Helicity silently echoed. Now everyone was working hard to stormproof the bed-and-breakfast. Afterward, they would pack their bags—Mia for her return flight to Michigan, Suze for a visit with friends away from the coast, and Helicity and Sam for their road trip with Andy. They all planned to leave as soon as humanly possible.

Helicity prayed Andy showed up in time. The sooner they hit the road the safer they would be.

"He knows," Helicity answered Suze's question. "He's with Johnny, finishing up some last-minute . . . business." She waited for Suze to drill a series of small holes down the edges of a large plywood board before adding, "I'm sorry he's not here to help."

"Fine time for him to vanish," Mia complained. "We need his muscle."

"What am I, chopped liver?" Sam hefted the board into place over a window.

Mia appraised the sinewy muscles of his bare back

and arms and shrugged. "Meh. I guess you'll do."

Helicity wanted to join in their banter. But her uneasiness made even smiling seem impossible.

The one bright spot of the day was when Trey showed up unexpectedly, laden with food for a last picnic on the beach. Helicity allowed herself to relax while they ate, but no longer.

"I'm sorry, Trey," she apologized when she saw his downcast expression. "It's just there's a ton to do, and I've got a lot on my mind." She touched his hand. "But I'm really glad you came over. I wasn't sure if I was going to have a chance to say good-bye in person."

"*Good-bye.*" Trey punched the sand over and over. "I hate that word."

"Me too."

They gathered up the remains of the meal, then headed back toward the Beachside.

"So, listen." Trey stopped her on the dune path. "I, um, I got you something. You know, to remember me by."

As always, Trey's awkward shyness spread warmth through her. "Trey," she said softly, "I'll always remember you. Always."

"Still." He pressed a small package into her hand. "I was going to give it to you at the lake that day. But we never got a chance to sail together." He made a face at the sky. "Thanks again for that, derecho."

Helicity giggled, then opened the package. Inside was a tiny glass-stoppered bottle containing a single piece of silver-blue dolphin confetti.

"It's the confetti from your party," Trey told her. "There's a little loop of wire so you can wear it as a necklace. If you want."

"I want." Helicity immediately threaded the bottle onto the chain that held Lana's lightning bolt. The two charms nestled together, metal and glass, gold and silver-blue. "It's beautiful and I love it."

She hesitated, then opened her arms and closed the distance between them. Trey enveloped her in a lingering hug and for a moment, Helicity felt happy. Then he pulled back. But he didn't release her. Instead, he touched the side of her face and slowly moved in until his lips were so close to hers she could feel the heat coming from his breath.

A car horn honked, signaling his mother's arrival. Trey didn't let that stop him. His other hand brushed her cheek. And then he pressed his lips to hers.

It was her first kiss. She blinked her eyes open, breathed Trey in, and tried to cherish it. To give herself over to it. But for some reason, she held back. Why, she didn't know. It was a beautiful kiss. At least she thought it was. Especially for a first kiss. Not that she would know any different. And yet . . .

Trey sensed her detachment. He pulled away from the kiss and opened his eyes. She read confusion, then hurt in their dark depths. Without saying a word, he turned and ran to the car. The door slammed, and he was gone.

She blinked back tears of guilt as she watched his car disappear around a bend. As she headed up the Beachside stairs, her anxiety about the kiss melted into the anxiety over Andy again, and with it, a new feeling of guilt.

"I shouldn't have confronted him like that," she berated herself later that afternoon as she and Sam packed the camping gear into the trunk of his car. "Now he's out there somewhere with Johnny. Or worse, alone and—and . . ." She couldn't finish the thought.

Johnny's warning about withdrawal had haunted her after she went to bed the night before. Unable to sleep, she looked it up on her phone. The list of symptoms was appalling. Nausea and vomiting. Fever. Racing heart. Muscle cramps. Depression. Agitation. And worst of all, an overpowering craving for drugs.

She didn't regret throwing Mia's pills in the ocean. But the thought of her brother suffering because of what she'd done or turning to desperate measures to feed his craving . . . it was almost more than she could bear. And his continued absence added fuel to the fire of her rising panic.

So did the hurricane now spiraling into the Gulf. Two days earlier, the tropical storm—as it had been then—had lashed Jamaica, the Cayman Islands, and the south coast of Cuba with the heavy rain and damaging winds. Since then, it had traveled on a northwest track toward the Gulf, sucking up energy from the warm tropical waters and mushrooming to a Category-1 and now to a Cat-2 with a well-defined eye, outer bands that stretched out nearly three hundred miles, and wind speeds clocked by aircraft reconnaissance at ninety-eight miles per hour. It was still several hundred miles from the Texas coast. But it was coming closer.

For those who knew what to look for, the signs of the hurricane's approach were clear. Increased winds. Mounting waves. Cirrus clouds building on the horizon. Helicity saw it all while on the beach with Trey. She knew what would come next. By late afternoon, the clouds would have thickened, and the winds and waves would be blowing and surging with greater power.

If they were lucky, that would be the worst to happen for many hours yet, and their planned departure that night would be without risk. The storm was moving at a decent clip of sixteen miles per hour last she checked, but storms often slowed before making landfall. She hoped this one would, too, because they were running out of time to escape, and still, no Andy.

The size of the hurricane was also troubling. Many people believed a hurricane was only dangerous when it made landfall. But the truth was, the outer bands could be treacherous, too. Their spiraling winds could whip up tornadoes and spawn destructive thunderstorms with heavy rain, fierce wind gusts, and damaging lightning. Coastal communities could experience significant flooding while the center of the hurricane was still hundreds of miles away.

The only certainty with hurricanes, Lana had once told Helicity, was that each was unique. Getting out of the storm's path before it was in striking distance was always the best option. And that's just what Helicity intended to do.

But not without Andy.

CHAPTER TWENTY-SIX

"This is not how I wanted to say good-bye."

Helicity looked up from Sam's car to see Suze was trundling down the front stairs with a suitcase in each hand. Mia was right behind her with her own luggage.

"Me neither," Mia added miserably as she loaded her belongings into Suze's hybrid sedan. "But if we don't leave now, we'll miss my flight."

Helicity bit her lip. Mia's flight home wasn't until nine that night. On a good day, she and Suze could have left two hours later and still made it to the airport with plenty of time to spare.

It was far from a good day. While they'd been battening down the Beachside and packing, the hurricane had ballooned to a Cat-3. All reports indicated it was growing even stronger, and while the outer bands weren't expected to hit for another hour or so, carloads of anxious people were already streaming onto the main highway off the peninsula in droves.

A sudden gust of wind tossed Suze's hair into her face. She pushed it aside impatiently, then fixed Helicity with a troubled stare. "I don't like leaving you here alone."

"She's not alone." Sam slammed his car trunk and came to stand beside Helicity. "And we're only hanging around until Andy gets back. Then believe me, we are hitting the road."

"When *is* he getting here?" Mia wanted to know.

"Pretty soon," Helicity said vaguely.

Suze held her gaze for a moment longer. Then she turned to Sam and folded him into a hug. "You are always welcome here, my friend. And listen: you take care of her. And yourself."

"I will," Sam promised.

Suze let go and faced Helicity. "Your parents are very lucky people to have a daughter like you. And Mia is even luckier to have you in her life."

"Totally," Mia agreed with heartfelt conviction.

Helicity tried to thank Suze, but the words caught in her throat. Instead, she threw her arms around her in a tight hug.

"Come back anytime," Suze whispered in her ear. "Your room will be waiting."

Helicity hugged Mia even more fiercely. "See you at home in a few days."

"Yeah. We'll go back-to-school shopping. Yippee yay," Mia said with mock enthusiasm.

Helicity smiled as they hugged one more time. Then Mia and Suze climbed into the car, Suze started the engine, and they drove off.

Helicity's smile faded when she turned back to the Beachside and saw Sam's frown. "Still nothing from Andy?" he asked.

She checked both her phone and her brother's and shook her head.

He glanced at the sky and scanned the thickening

clouds overhead. His frown deepened. "I'm going to gas up the car. And I'm sorry, Fifteen, but when I get back, we're leaving, Andy or no Andy."

Helicity sucked in her breath. "What? No!"

He took a step toward her. "Remember our pact? And the promise I just made to Suze? Well, I'm keeping both and getting us out of here safely."

"But—"

Sam silenced her with a finger to her lips. It was a featherlight touch, but it sent a shock wave through her system. She stopped breathing. He stared down at her for a moment longer, as if daring her to speak. She held his gaze unwaveringly. Defiantly.

His look changed to something softer then. Warmer. His finger shifted, and he traced a line across her mouth and down beneath her chin. Time suddenly seemed to stand still as he tilted her face upward. Then he leaned forward, and softly, gently, touched his lips to hers.

Helicity didn't even have time to close her eyes. She was stunned, her eyes still locked with his.

"Be back soon, Fifteen," he whispered. Then he pulled away, got into his car, and roared off.

Helicity climbed the stairs to the kitchen in a dream, barely registering that the wind was buffeting her with every step. Inside the house, things looked completely different. The view of the Gulf through the picture windows had been replaced by a wall of plywood boards. Stacks of Adirondack chairs from the deck and fire pit clogged the common room. The bicycles leaned against the hallway wall, and the Boogie Boards and other beach gear sat in forlorn piles here and there. The whole place had a melancholy feel of abandonment. The only spot of brightness was a sun-drenched shot of the Bolivar lighthouse—one of Sam's photographs, she knew.

Suze had told them earlier to take whatever food and drinks they wanted for their ride. Helicity was stuffing granola bars, apples, and bottles of water into her backpack when her phone suddenly buzzed. Her heart leaped into her throat. Someone was trying to video chat with her. It wasn't a number she recognized, but if there was even a chance it was Andy . . .

She hit ACCEPT. At first, the screen showed nothing but a distortion. Then a shadowy figure in a hoodie appeared.

"Andy?" she whispered.

"Hel . . ."

Helicity let out a sob. "Andy! Are you okay? Where are you?"

"Someplace safe."

He didn't say anything else for a long minute. She tried to see his face, to connect with his eyes. But he must have moved his hand because the picture shifted abruptly. She caught a quick glimpse of his surroundings. A wide-open expanse of patchy grass. Palm trees. A building on stilts in the background. Something about the area looked familiar, but before she could identify the location, Andy came back into view.

"Andy!" she cried. "Listen, just tell me where you are. Sam and I will come get you."

"No. Stay away from me."

He looked so tortured, sounded so defeated, her heart nearly broke. "That's not going to happen, but I need to know where to find you," she pleaded.

Andy hesitated. Then he scrubbed his face with his hand and looked directly into the camera. "I'm—"

Suddenly, a ferocious blast of wind rocked the

Beachside on its stilts. Startled, Helicity dropped the phone and clutched the island countertop with both hands. She recovered after a second. But when she picked up the phone, Andy was gone.

"No, no, no, no, no!" She stabbed her finger at the screen, desperately trying to reestablish the connection. But her attempts bounced right back. *Message failed. No signal. Message failed.* She got the same results when she tried Sam.

Frustrated by her helplessness, she paced the room like a caged animal, her eyes darting from the stacked chairs to the beach gear before landing on Sam's photograph. She froze as she took in the full image. Not just the tall black tower, but its surroundings, too. An expanse of patchy grass. Palm trees. A building on stilts. Her eyes widened, and she gasped. "He's at the lighthouse!"

Her joy lasted only a second before reality hit. Yes, she knew where Andy had been when he called. But would he stay there, and for how long? Or would he disappear again before she could reach him?

Panic pulsed through her veins. She ran to the kitchen window, praying she'd see Sam pulling into the parking area. Nothing. Tried his phone again. No signal.

Outside, the wind howled. The thought of Andy alone out in the gathering storm . . .

"No," she said out loud. "I'm going to get him."

She looped her arms through her backpack straps and grabbed one of the bikes. The Bolivar lighthouse was just a short ride away. She could be there in no time. Then Sam could come get them. Or they'd walk back to the Beachside together. And if Andy refused to leave . . . well, she'd deal with that when she found him.

She dashed off a note to Sam explaining where she was, then muscled the bike down the stairs. Moments later, she was pedaling furiously along the main road. A long line of cars, all headed in the opposite direction, stretched in front and behind her. Some honked as she passed. A few people yelled at her that she was going the wrong way. A snarling dog lunged at her through an open window, making her swerve sharply. But she didn't stop, not even when the wind gust threatened to blow her off the road into a ditch.

Hold on, Andy. I'm coming.

CHAPTER TWENTY-SEVEN

"**S**hoot!"

Helicity was pedaling so hard against the headwind she missed the turnoff to the lighthouse. She wheeled about, bouncing painfully as the smooth pavement gave way to the more rugged asphalt of the side road. She rose up in her seat and pushed on. The road to the lighthouse was isolated—just fields, trees, and marshy pools of water—and straight as an arrow until the very end. Eyes trained on the black tower on the stormy horizon, she swept around the curve—and nearly crashed into a metal gate blocking the entrance.

Swearing, she skidded to a stop. Attached to the gate was a handful of signs, all of which said essentially the same thing: PRIVATE PROPERTY. NO TRESPASSING.

She hesitated.

I've come this far, she thought. *I'm not leaving until I've looked for him.*

Like the Beachside, the two houses adjacent to the lighthouse were boarded up. There was no sign of movement anywhere on the property and no cars in sight. The owners appeared to have left ahead of the storm. But what about Andy?

She maneuvered the bike through an opening in a hedge next to the gate and dropped it and her backpack near an electric pole. Feeling like a criminal, she hurried across the grass to the first house, crept up the stairs, and tried the doorknob. It was locked. She listened carefully. Except for the wind, the only sound was the persistent clang from a nearby flagpole. She moved on to the second house. Same thing.

That left the lighthouse. From far away, its cast-iron panels looked black, but up close they were the reddish brown of years-old rust. The tower loomed several stories above her. A wide wooden platform circled the top like the brim of a hat. Above that was the enclosure from which the brilliant beacon used to shine.

"Andy?" she called as she circled the base looking for a way in. "Andy, are you here?"

Any doubts that she was in the right place disappeared when she found the door. It was the one from Andy's phone—a rusty metal slab with an X riveted to the front. In the photo, it had been padlocked shut. But someone had busted open the lock. Recently, she guessed, when she spied a chunk of concrete lying half hidden in the grass.

She laid her hand on the door and was about to push it open when something occurred to her. What if the person who'd broken the lock was inside—and what if that person wasn't Andy?

You can't chicken out now, she scolded herself. *Go in.*

With silent apologies to the owners for trespassing, she gave the door a shove. It swung open easily, startling her when it banged against the wall. She took a deep breath and stepped inside.

The air was cooler inside the tower and smelled faintly dank, the way the basement in her old house had before her father converted it into a man cave. She detected a whiff of bird droppings, too. Natural light probably filtered in when the sun was shining, but right now, it was so dim she could only make out vague shapes. She thumbed her phone to flashlight mode, squinting for a moment against the sudden glare.

Unlike the black metal exterior, the interior walls were made of whitewashed brick, pockmarked and scuffed with age. Spiraling up through the center was an iron staircase with narrow, open-backed treads and a skinny iron handrail bolted to the wall. Arched doorways led to small rooms off the main entrance. A few steps in was a shallow storage area with wooden shelves canted at odd angles. She shivered, remembering the shelves in the derelict cabin that had lifted the tree off Trey's leg.

A scuffling noise from above rocketed her back to the present. Her free hand crept to her lightning bolt necklace, now paired with Trey's keepsake. "Andy?"

The noise stopped. She aimed her phone light

upward and craned her neck to peer up the stairs. But the light only reached so far. If it was Andy up there, she couldn't see him. And maybe he didn't want her to.

No. Stay away from me, he'd said.

"Not going to happen," she muttered.

With the phone in one hand and her other hand grasping the rail, she began to climb. Her footfalls tapped out hollow tones on the old metal steps. She hadn't realized how thick the walls were until she passed a small landing that tunneled horizontally for several feet before ending in a tiny window. She couldn't see anything through the window. But from the continuous moan of the wind, she imagined the outer bands of the hurricane were inching closer by the minute.

She picked up her pace. One circuit above the landing, she heard the scuffling again. She paused and shone her phone straight up, trying to identify the sound's source.

She gasped when the light flashed onto a pale white face. Two piercing black eyes stared down at her. Before she could comprehend what she was seeing, there was a bone-chilling screech and the face streaked down at her with unbelievable speed.

With a cry of terror, she flung up her arms. The sudden violence of her movement jerked her off balance. As she flailed for the railing, her hand smacked into a step. Her phone went flying, its beam of light whirling crazily as it ricocheted down the stairs. Then the phone shattered on the floor and the light winked out, plunging her into gloomy darkness.

Clutching the railing and breathing heavily, she pressed her back against the wall and willed her wildly thumping heart to slow.

"It was just an owl," she whispered. "Just an owl."

And it was likely the owl, not Andy, that had made the scuffling sounds. Even now, she could hear the bird settling back into its roost. No doubt it knew exactly where she was, too. She wondered if it would attack her again if she continued up the stairs.

So . . . keep going? Or turn back?

The sudden sound of rain drumming against the tower walls decided it for her. She'd come here to find her brother. No bird was going to stop her.

She pulled Andy's phone from her back pocket,

flicked it to flashlight mode, and cautiously moved the beam toward the owl's roost. She made sure not to shine it directly on the owl itself, but the bird still fluffed out its feathers and hooted a warning. It didn't move, though, which she took as a good sign.

She shifted the beam to the space above it. The light shone through several more loops of staircase before landing on a steep metal ladder. The ladder led to a small trapdoor set in a metal platform—the brim of the hat circling the top of the lighthouse. The door was closed. But if there was even a chance Andy had crawled through it to the platform . . .

Keep going.

With one eye on the owl and one hand on the railing, she pushed off from the wall. Step-by-step, she climbed higher into the lighthouse. The walls slowly closed in as the tower narrowed, and at one turn she felt the railing pull free from the bricks. She swallowed hard then, wanting but not daring to call out to Andy, not with that bird following her every movement with its keen stare. With the wind howling louder every second, he might not have heard her anyway.

At the next landing, she risked a look down—and immediately snapped her eyes upward again. She wasn't afraid of heights, but the ground looked very far away.

Three more circuits, and the stairs would end at the ladder. But first, she'd have to pass the owl's roost. She wished she had a weapon of some sort. Not to hurt the bird, just to fend it off if it swooped at her.

Her heart pounded in her chest as she drew nearer the roost. Sweat prickled on her scalp and in her armpits. Out of nowhere, a nature show about how predators could sense fear flashed through her mind. She shoved the memory aside even as she edged away from the outer wall to put as much distance between herself and the owl as possible. She was forced to walk on her tiptoes now, for close to the central post the triangular treads narrowed to a blunt point. Her free hand stayed curled around the railing, steadying her more than pulling her forward.

One more circuit and she'd be face-to-face with the owl. *I can do—*

BRAAANG!

An earsplitting ring shattered the air just as she was

taking a step. She cried out in terror as her foot slipped off the tread and plunged into nothingness. Her hand instinctively tightened around the railing, and she swung backward into the wall, hitting it so hard the air was knocked out of her lungs.

Then all hell broke loose.

The piercing ring came again, startling the owl. Screeching, it swooped down at her. Talons raised and powerful wings beating at her face, it trapped her against the bricks. Too terrified to even scream, she struck out at it with both hands. Its sharp claws tore a gash in her arm before she landed a blow that sent the bird flapping off. Sobbing, her hands trembling and blood dripping from her arm, she scooted down the stairs, putting as much distance as she could between her and the owl's roost.

BRAAANG!

She finally registered that the ring was coming from Andy's phone. Sam's number flared on the tiny screen. With another sob, this time of relief, she sank down onto a step and swiped to answer it.

"Sam?"

"Fifteen!" Sam boomed out. "Finally! Listen, I

found Andy! We're on our way—" There was a crackling sound and his voice cut out.

"Sam? *Sam?*" she cried.

"—stuck in traffic! It's taking forever to—" There was more crackling. And then there was nothing.

"Sam!" she shrieked. But it was no good. The signal was lost. For the first time in hours, though, hope wasn't. Sam had found Andy. They were on their way to the Beachside. She had to be there when they arrived.

"I'm coming, Andy!" She jammed the phone in her back pocket, grabbed hold of the railing, and started to yank herself up. "Sam, I'm—"

With a rasp of metal against crumbling mortar, the railing bolt suddenly pulled away from the wall. Helicity pitched forward, still clinging to the rod. Her arm twisted awkwardly behind her. Then the railing snapped to a halt, wrenching her shoulder nearly out of its socket.

With a scream of agony, she let go. Her foot caught on a step and she plummeted down the stairs. Her head cracked against the bricks. The last thing she remembered before everything went black was the blaring ring from Andy's phone.

CHAPTER TWENTY-EIGHT

The sound of running water. Of howling wind and on-again, off-again knocking. Dull, thudding pain in her shoulder. In her head. A stinging sensation on her arm.

Helicity slit her eyes open and was met with utter blackness. She opened them wider, trying to make sense of the impenetrable dark. Then out of the ink, or maybe it was from the darkness of her mind, came a whispered voice.

"Don't give up. Don't give up. Don't give up."

Lana's voice. An image exploded in her mind of Lana mouthing the words as they struggled against the pull of the flood. It was so real, Helicity swore she could feel that water lapping at her limbs, dragging at her clothes, its saltiness seeping into her bones.

No, her fogged brain resisted. *That's not possible. The flood was before. That water was fresh. This water is from something else.*

Somewhere beyond, a low moan rose into a shriek, growing louder and sharper with every pulse of her throbbing head. Fear impaled her innards and suddenly, her mouth filled with saliva. She rocked sideways, felt the sharp stab of pain in her shoulder, then heaved and vomited up her stomach's sour contents. The taste of bile brought with it a moment of clarity.

Andy. I was looking for Andy.

Clutching her aching arm at the elbow, she struggled to sit up. Her fingers brushed the rough floor, and like a bolt of lightning, she remembered.

The hurricane. The railing. The pain.

She lifted her hand and gingerly touched her head. There was a lump—a goose egg, her mother would have called it—and her fingers came away sticky. She swallowed hard. *Blood.*

The memories were coming in clearer pictures now. She was inside the lighthouse. She'd fallen down the stairs, all the way to the floor from what she could tell. She touched her shoulder and winced. She feared she'd dislocated it, but after a few tentative rolls, she decided that while painful, it was intact.

But how long had she been out? Why hadn't Sam and Andy come to find her? And where had all this water come from?

She fumbled for Andy's phone. Soaked in seawater, it was dead. She rolled to her knees and crawled forward through the sloshing wet to where she thought the lighthouse door ought to be. The howling and shrieking grew louder the closer she got, the sound knifing into her skull. She felt the wind as it whistled through holes in the door.

Something outside rapped against the metal. She recoiled, startled, then licked her lips and tried her voice. "Hello?" she called hoarsely. "Is someone out there?"

There was no answer.

She shifted her position and pressed her eye to a hole.

Outside the door was a world locked in the throes of raging chaos. Surging seawater and torrential rain drowned the land in all directions. Wind and waves pounded the toppled houses into kindling. Winds so strong they bent palm trees as easily as licorice sticks ripped the road gate from the ground, and snapped at least one electric pole in half. She stared at the dangling wires in horror before realizing they must be dead.

She squeezed her eyes shut and felt for her necklace. Miraculously, it had survived the fall. As she clutched it, she thought about flinging open the door and fleeing her prison. But she resisted the urge. As horrifying as it was to be trapped alone inside the lighthouse, it was infinitely safer here than out there.

Hours of hungrily researching weather had taught her that the power of water was like nothing else. Storm surge could move entire buildings and homes from their foundations. Debris hidden within the rushing water could mow down people like a runaway locomotive. One wrong step, and you could be swept away. She didn't need a book to know that. Her own experience had taught her as much.

Bam!

The sudden sound of a large object ricocheting off the door broke her out of her reverie. She realized with a start that the rising water had swallowed her thighs and was creeping steadily up to her waist.

I have to get to higher ground.

Another crash rocked the tower as she slogged over to the spiral staircase. Her shoulder and her head screaming with pain, she began to climb. Or rather, to crawl, dragging herself up one tread to the next on her hands and knees.

To stop her mind from spinning out of control, she thought about the story Mia had told her, about the 120 people who had sheltered in this same lighthouse during the 1900 hurricane. It staggered her to imagine the terrified men, women, and children crushed together on these steps. Had they screamed in terror? Clung to one another for strength—or channeled their fear by lashing out? Suddenly, she was glad to be trapped here alone. She pushed away the images and focused on the positive: they'd all survived.

Halfway up, she paused, straining her ears for any sign of the owl. But it must have flown off, for there was no warning screech, no attack. She considered stopping for good then. There was no reason to continue, after all. She was safe there on the stairs.

Or so she thought until more debris blasted the lighthouse. The hit shook loose several bricks high above her. They rained down around her, narrowly missing her head as she cowered against the wall. As painful as it was to keep going, staying put no longer seemed like the best option.

After endless, torturous minutes of climbing, she reached the ladder. Exhausted, she wanted nothing more than to lie down and sleep. But the cramped area offered no place to sit, let alone stretch out. The platform beyond the trapdoor, though, promised both.

Up close, that small door reminded her of one from her favorite book, *Alice in Wonderland*. Alice was much too big to fit through her door until she drank a magic potion that shrank her down to the right size. Helicity had no magic potion. She prayed she'd fit through her door without it.

It took every ounce of energy left in her body to

begin that final climb. Toes marching in the air and her good arm screaming with effort, she boosted herself up rung after rung. She wrapped her bad arm around the top and pushed on the door with the other.

It didn't budge. She choked back a sob. That the trap might be too heavy for her to move had never occurred to her.

No. I will *open it.*

She took a deep breath and tried again. With a groan, it lifted an inch. She gave a mighty shove, and the door flew open and landed on the platform with a bang. The roar of the wind and the thud of rain had been loud before, but now, with the door open, it was deafening. She climbed two more rungs and stuck her head through the opening.

The tower continued up to meet a newer wooden platform with another hatch accessed by another ladder. The two landings with the protected space between reminded Helicity of a sandwich cookie.

At the thought of cookies, Helicity's stomach suddenly contracted. Water dripping through cracks in the wooden platform and running in rivulets down the brick walls made her throat ache with thirst. She berated herself for not bringing her supply-stuffed backpack with her to the lighthouse. Both it and the bicycle had undoubtedly been swept away hours ago.

"I can't do anything about food," she muttered. "But I can drink rainwater."

With that goal in mind, she heaved herself up onto the platform, lay on her back, and opened her mouth to capture drops from the steadiest drip. The water tasted funny, but it soothed her thirst, so she didn't care. She caught some in her hands and rubbed it on her face to fight off the wave of exhaustion urging her to sleep. But sleep and concussions don't mix. So instead, she stared up at the wooden platform and listened to the storm raging around her.

After a few minutes, she sat up, cocked her head to the side, and listened more closely. Maybe it was just her imagination or wishful thinking, but—

The rain. The wind. They're not as strong as before.

Her drowsiness vanished. Minutes ticked by. The rain lightened from a thrumming drumbeat to a gentle tapping, then ceased altogether. The howl of the wind was replaced by a distant and constant *whoosh-thump* that Helicity recognized as the crash and roll of waves.

The eye. I'm in the eye of the hurricane, she thought wonderingly.

The hatch in the wooden platform proved easier to open. Above, she was greeted by a clear night sky studded with stars and a sliver of a moon. Warm fresh air kissed by rain and the scent of the sea filled her nostrils. It was so beautiful, so eerily peaceful, she could almost believe she'd dreamed the hurricane.

Then she looked down, and reality punched her in the face.

Where land and life had been just hours before, now there was nothing but filthy water clogged with debris for as far as her eye could see. Even from this height she could pick out a half-submerged car with a shattered windshield. An overturned boat, its keel rocking in the waves. A waterlogged easy chair slowly rotating in an unseen current. The roofs and walls, studs and stilts of ruined houses drifting together in clumps like jumbled toy kits waiting to be pieced together. And trash. Thick blankets of the stuff floated everywhere.

Staring at the horror below, she realized how incredibly lucky she was. If she'd been caught outside in the hurricane . . .

She sucked in her breath. *Andy. Sam.*

They'd been together before the storm hit. But where were they now? Safe on the mainland? Or somewhere in the horrifying debris-filled soup below?

And what did they think had happened to her?

Her heart cried out in anguish then. She fell to her knees, racked with sobs for several long minutes. Then a puff of wind made her look up.

The eye of the hurricane was passing. And in its wake would follow the other side of the hurricane, part of the eye wall, and with it, more deadly winds, torrential rain, and storm surge. Until it passed, she was trapped in her black tower.

That knowledge should have filled her with desperation. But it was as if her tears had washed away her fears, for as she gazed out toward the horizon where the next onslaught would appear, she felt a calm determination settle over her.

This lighthouse has survived worse, she thought. *And so have I. So, go ahead and come at me, hurricane.*

She captured her necklace in her hand. *I'm ready.*